PUFFIN
ISLAND

By

Sherry Schubert

Published by Sunway Press
P.O. Box 5825
Twin Falls, Idaho 83303-5825
mcallistersh@yahoo.com

Cover image by Molly Jayne McAllister

ISBN 978-0-9829563-0-4 (ebook)
ISBN 978-0-9829563-1-1   (pbk)

For

My Children

Acknowledgments
Claudia Creek for her buoyant support and assistance
Mark McAllister for his sound criticism and factual acuity
Molly McAllister for her encouragement
to follow my passion

Books by Sherry Schubert
Puffin Island
Celtic Compass, Part I
Celtic Compass, Part II
Celtic Circle~for Better, for Worse
Celtic Circle~Forever

Puffin Island

Prologue

Paula's search began innocently enough with a computer, a list of names and a web address. Her first foray into the internet world of social networking was intended to be an interesting diversion, a learning exercise of sorts. Encouraged by her adult children to accept the intrusiveness of 21st century communications as inevitable, she thought this list would make an interesting, if not fruitful, search. Was the impetus for such a query an effort to clear away the remnants of her life before her children were left with that responsibility, or was it an attempt to summon the memories of her bygone past before they faded completely? She was not sure, but the fact that this list remained in her old travel journal after all these years must be a sign that providence would smile on her investigation.

In no particular order, Paula entered the names and the vitals she remembered:

Name: Bo Wijnbladh
Country: Sweden
DoB: @1950.
Unknown. Hmm. He must not have been as remarkable as she thought at the time.

Name: James McMahon
Country: Thurso, Caithness, Scotland.
DoB: @1933.
Nuclear engineer. Author/publisher of several works relating to northern Scotland. Deceased: 2005. Paula recalled his own self-description, "...of Anglo-Saxon extraction but not extracted enough," as they extricated themselves from a 3,000 year old burial cairn on the moors.

Name: Richard Moon
Country: England.
DoB: @1917.
British free-lance photographer, contributor to such publications as the *London Times*, *Daily Telegraph* and *Daily Mirror*. Deceased: 1983. An exploration of links to these publications revealed nothing beyond the newsworthy. Thank goodness his discretion prevailed in the days before his entire portfolio would have been spread bare across the Internet!

Paul and Sadie Humphries: Deceased.
Margie Morimoto: Unknown.
John and Gudrin Reichert: Unknown.
Nancy McNamara: Unknown.

Name: Bata Karninsha
Country: Rijeka,Yugoslavia (It was still Yugoslavia then.)
DoB: @1930.
Yugolinia Sea Captain. Deceased: 1993. Victim of a brutal ethnic war? He was so proud of being a "Bosnian Man" that he would give up the sea to defend his ancestral home without a second thought.

Name: Martin Maxson
Country: Massachusetts, U. S. A.
DoB: 1945.
B.A. Harvard. Art History 1967. Deceased: 1969. Another victim of another war. He received the forwarding of his draft notice in Paris. They met on Paula's first visit there. He seemed to know he would not return as they shared a final tearful walk along the river, wending their way back and forth across its bridges.

Name: Nicholas Dean Conyers
Country: London, England
DoB: @1935.
British reporter, foreign correspondent, *The Daily Telegraph*. Deceased: 1993. Paula's heart lurched at the finality of her rebound foreign liaison. How could Nick be dead for so long and she not feel it? His death at a relatively young age was not particularly surprising for he smoked continuously and enjoyed a "hard life" by his own admission, but the fact of his passing left her empty for a moment. Without a waver, she followed the link to his paper's archives and accessed numerous articles he wrote, noticing that there were submissions right up to the year he died. Not surprising, for without his words Nick's life would have been nothing.

Paula ran her fingers across the screen atop his byline. She knew it well; he spelled it out for the overseas operator nearly every day. They spent most days together writing during the summer of '69: he for the paper and she in her journal. The cramped garret they shared on an unpretentious *rue* in Paris had barely room enough for one workspace, certainly not two. While Nick used the desk to type his stories about student unrest or the Paris/Vietnam peace talks, Paula sat on the bed and scribbled her notes. Then when he dictated his stories to the home office, she took her place at the typewriter and turned her notes into articles of observation and short stories. (Perhaps that is what spurred this investigation—the rereading of some of those stories as she packed them away... again.) She remembered him most readily reciting for the operator, "C—O—N—e-grec—uh—ere—S." When she thought of Nick, even now, that sound is what came to her mind first, not his name nor his face. To suggest that they shared a garret, competitiveness on the chessboard, a love of the written word and nothing more would be folly. When he was called back to London after several months together, the last night they shared brought the realization and reluctant acceptance that this was the proverbial "The End;" there would be no more pages of their *histoire* to turn. Nick's death now confirmed that.

Paula hesitated and drew a deep breath before entering the name she had saved for last, fearful of what she might discover.

Name: Thomas Michael Eamon O'Connell
Country: Dublin, Ireland
DoB: July 25, 1943.
Producer/director for Ireland's national radio/television service.

BINGO!

Sherry Schubert

Chapter 1

No, not true, Paula thought as she turned off the computer. *This search* did begin innocently with a computer, a list and a web address, but *their story* began some forty years ago in the aftermath of the "Summer of Love." The highways and byways of Europe were crowded with young Americans "hitching" their ways across that continent, packs on their backs and thumbs in the air, in an attempt to avoid the war, escape the war or deny that it was even happening. Paula traveled alone and without plan, unusual for a young single woman in 1968. She recently cast her first vote, absentee, for Bobby Kennedy in the California primary election and then learned that it was irrevocably erased by his assassination. In the wake of violence used to change the course of history once again, she sought a place of comfort. Her admiration for the Kennedy brothers made Ireland a fitting destination for the next leg of her travels.

What was not fitting was the rain—buckets and buckets of it pelting down from the sky as Paula found herself between rides on an unexpectedly isolated road leading to County Kerry. With a poncho at the bottom of her pack and an umbrella somewhere in Germany, she was too miserable to admire the varied shades of green surrounding her. She was Colorado farm girl enough to know that only constant irrigation would result in such lushness, and she was experiencing nature's way first hand. She kept her eyes trained on the roadway approaching from the east.

Three vehicles appeared on the horizon: a sports car, a sedan and a van. Paula dismissed the two-seater as improbable. The couple in the sedan or the workman in the van were much more likely to take pity on her, if past experience were any guide. Either one would have adequate room and be more inclined to rescue a damsel in distress and her soggy accoutrements. She wiped the hair from her eyes, put on a smile, extended her thumb… and blinked in astonishment as all three whizzed by!

With a stomp and an epithet, Paula turned back east again… to wait… for the "friendly" Irish to live up to their reputation. She detected the approach of a vehicle from behind and was surprised when it zoomed by, swerved around and came to a screeching stop beside her. It was the sports car, a sleek blue one, which just passed her up. The passenger door swung open and a friendly face with a pair of dancing eyes and two-days' growth beard beckoned her in.

"I cannot believe those others did not stop; they certainly had room! Not a very good advertisement for Irish hospitality, I'd say. It will be a bit of a cramp, but you are welcome to pile in if you think you can fit—with your pack and all, I mean."

The driver's voice had the lilt, but his appearance did not immediately shout "Irishman." His hair was brown, not the red she expected; it was neither coarse nor curly, just wavy. Hollow cheeks gave way to a square jaw and rounded chin with a hint of cleft barely evident beneath the stubble. A prominent brow ridge protected the expressive eyes which attracted her first. He was wearing clean but well-worn sweats and canvas slip-ons with no socks. His uncalloused hands had wide palms but slender fingers. His fine watch and professional manner made him seem older than the twenty-five years he later admitted.

Paula shuddered at her own appearance: trekking pants muddied around the cuffs, a damp matching sweater with T-shirt underneath, and heavy brown walking shoes just beginning to squish. A few errant ringlets escaped her kerchief and were stuck in wet curls to her face.

The smell of expensive leather overwhelmed her as she started to step into the car. Thanking the driver profusely, she displayed a wide full mouth surrounded by a magnificent smile and lost no time in taking the *Irish Times* newspaper from the passenger seat, opening it out to cover the upholstery and the floor. She noticed the man wince as she did; he probably had not read it yet, and she scolded herself for not asking first. She removed her bedroll from its plastic cover and folded both along the seat to sop up the rainwater she was obviously going to bring along with her into his prized auto.

The soggy hiker clambered in and pulled her pack into the small space left on her lap between her body and the dashboard, leaving her barely able to nod her head in effusive thanks again. "I can't tell you how grateful I am that you stopped. I'm headed for the Youth Hostel on Valentia Island and was beginning to think I'd be washed out to sea without a hot shower first." Reaching to shake his hand, she announced, "I'm Paula. From America. And you are…?"

"Tom," he replied, and was taken aback as soon as he said it. He was "Thomas" to his family: his father now dead two years, his widowed mother and four sisters, his aunts, uncles and cousins too numerous to name, and to most of his friends. He was "Mr. O'Connell" to those of new or recent acquaintance, business associates, his staff at home and at the station, and to anyone with whom his friends tried to "fix him up." As a boy on the island he was "Master Thomas," but when he crossed the threshold into long pants and adulthood he became "Mr. Thomas." He was "Tom" only to his most intimate friends and wondered how that familiar moniker escaped him so quickly and to a completely unknown female from five thousand miles distant, no less.

"You have relatives here? Friends?" Tom continued. Shaking her head in the negative led him to exclaim the obvious. "You can't be travelling alone!"

Paula nodded and reached into a side pocket of her pack. With only her right hand able to grope, she wrestled out a pencil and notebook, opened it to a well-worn page and jotted a hash mark alongside many others. Tom's quizzical look at her struggle invited an explanation. "I try to keep track of how many times I'm asked that question," she laughed. He did too.

As they sped toward the west coast and the spectacular Ring of Kerry, they exchanged particulars comfortably. Tom's job as a television producer of newscasts and documentaries made him more the interviewer and Paula the friendly subject. She did find out that he had an aunt who lived near the island, and he was taking a three-day holiday to check up on her as he did about four weekends a year.

"Hard to find time away from the office, you know. Always something breaking. Czechoslovakia is about to explode, and those bloody American students are spreading their contagion over here. Berkeley, Columbia University and now Paris; riots... and strikes." Apology leapt from his mouth. "I'm so sorry. I didn't mean to imply...."

"You may not have meant it, but you did use a rather broad generalization just now, and an accomplished newsman should know better," Paula teased gently. "Not all American college students are political science majors with a tendency toward protest or are communists as the California governor contends. Some just try to get an education and others, to avoid the draft. And I'm not about to tell you which side of *that* fence I'm on. I need this ride!" Paula smiled.

Tom did too, although he asked himself why he took her rebuke so lightly. He deserved it, of course; his remarks were uncalled for. But no young women of his acquaintance in Dublin would be so blunt.

He continued his interrogation cautiously and learned that his passenger graduated from Berkeley the previous year. Mortified by his earlier brazen comment, he skipped the question about her major. She worked while going to school, as was not usually done, to finance a trip to Europe and parts beyond before she returned to graduate school. Her eight-month trek through seventeen countries, countless museums and castles, and untallied pubs convinced her that she needed a repeat of all those classes she yawned through to truly appreciate what she attempted to absorb now.

If frugal, Paula could remain abroad for about another year. She hitchhiked and stayed at youth hostels whenever possible for the sake of economy. She was very thankful that the recent bestseller *Europe on Five Dollars a Day* overestimated necessities. She survived on about $3.50, less trains and ferries, but it was truly sometimes mere survival. She planned to stay a day or two at the Valentia hostel, depending on how interesting she found the island. She thanked him again for his kindness in helping her along this leg of her journey. Having slept in a jail outside Amsterdam, under a park bench in the rain in Folkestone, and at a home for wayward mothers in Smethwick, the prospect of a hot shower and clean bed up ahead was ideal.

Tom asked how and why Paula had come so far from her home in America. The "why" was easy because she repeated it so often. She wanted to give life to her studies, of course, but her primary goal was to gain some perspective. She felt that America was an "Everyman" in the world with its hodge-podge of diversity, traditions and tolerance for the most part. She wanted to see how it felt to be in a minority: the one who could not communicate through language, the one who could not read signs and had to ask for help from strangers, the one who was short on money and could not call home to be bailed out, the one who was white, the one who was stared at on a bus or in a church or just walking down the street because she looked different from everyone else. Swimming in a sea of strangers gave her a chance to try behaviors on for size to see which to practice until they became habits. Lastly, she hoped a newfound perspective would help her choose a graduate major from among several she was considering.

It was the "how" that astounded Tom. Paula crossed the Atlantic via Yugoslavian freighter. Had she no fear? "Aren't the Yugoslavs communists?" he asked.

"Yes," she replied, "but they explained that the only thing 'red' about them besides the color of their passports was the color of their blood, and when you're all *on* the same boat, you're all *in* the same boat, so to speak."

The ship carried about thirty passengers per crossing, solely to make extra money. On her voyage about half were an assortment of college students and other wandering waifs, while the remainder were Yugoslavs returning to the homeland with money for their families. The two groups did not mix much during the days, did not eat together although they shared the same Slavic menu, but they did sing and folk dance together in the evenings, traditional instruments providing the music.

Thus Paula developed an appreciation for this vibrant fun-loving people and intended to visit their country before she returned home.

She knew she would feel safe even though beyond the "Iron Curtain" because she received numerous invitations to stay with new friends and would not be on her own. Traveling by freighter was not really a choice; it was cheap, but a boon nonetheless and a great extension of her multicultural studies.

Tom's travel tales were not quite so unusual. He had visited most major European cities, usually to set up interviews or schedule filming for news documentaries. He would try to stay an extra day or two to see the sights but always felt pressed to get back to work. He never had the pleasure of voyaging on a freighter, but he did have a sailboat, his pride and joy. He cruised mostly on the Irish Sea and enjoyed putting in at small villages along the eastern coast. He had sailed since he was a boy. He learned right there in Valentia Harbor and on Portmagee Channel, about a half mile of sea between the island and mainland which was relatively calm in good weather. He also crewed on fishing boats during summers when he was a teenager. He preferred working at sea to partying in Dublin like many young men of privilege. That is how he knew most of the village folks around.

Somewhere along the way the rain stopped, but the two travelers did not notice. Easy conversation continued even as they crossed to the island on a small ferry and until they pulled up in front of the youth hostel. Paula let herself out of the car dragging pack and bedroll behind her. Then she tried to refold Tom's newspaper, but it would not behave. He gave her a "that is not necessary" look, so she closed the door, mouthed another thank you, and flashed him an engaging smile with her parting wave. He went on to his aunt's.

* * * * *

Aunt Moira's was not a long drive from the island, just a few kilometers across the channel actually, but it was long enough for Tom to ponder, while waiting for the ferry, just what impulse inspired him to do what he did. He never picked up hitchhikers, especially lone female ones. Irish girls would not be alone in a car with a strange man; Irish girls traveled in twos or threes wherever they went unless they were engaged. What was he thinking inviting all that rainwater onto his leather upholstery? His paper was ruined, but his seat was saved by her cleverness, he noticed. So, what was it about this girl that prompted him to do the unlikely?

Tom thought of his sister Anne and her friends finding themselves in a similar predicament. He imagined Anne's pout, her affront at being passed up, and her censure for anyone who did not think to come along the road sooner precisely to give her a lift! This girl, this Paula, had such a completely different attitude.   She displayed no air of entitlement or expectancy, no grumble at her condition, no glare of "it's about time!"   She was grateful, pleasant and casual even while being drenched, and she displayed the friendliest, most enchanting smile from the time she first entered his view until she was rescued and they were on their way again.   It was refreshing to be with a girl who would talk about something rather than giggle about nothing.

For the second time that day, on impulse, Tom turned his car around and headed in the opposite direction.

Chapter 2

Paula could not get into a shower fast enough. She was chilled to the bone and still dripping from the rain. First she had to check in, and found "Alfie," according to his nametag, behind the desk. When she handed him her registration and the required number of shillings, he said, "Well, Miss Paula from Colorado, welcome to Valentia Island. I see you've already met our Mr. O'Connell."

"Mr. O'Connell? Was it he who gave me the lift?"

" 'Twas, Miss. Everybody hereabouts knows his spiffy roadster."

"Does he stay here often?" she asked jokingly.

"He don't stay *here*, Miss. 'E's been comin' to these parts for as long as I can remember. Used to spend most o' the summers, but since 'e's growed up and workin' in the city, we don't see so much of 'im as we used to. Mr. Thomas comes over three or four times a year, though, to stay with his aunt over t' the mainland, just like the old days. T'check up on her, like. 'E's a nice young man, 'e is."

"Well, thank you, Alfie," Paula said thinking, that name is so Hollywood. "I've heard this is a really great hostel and I'm looking forward to a long, hot shower. I'm sorry I've tracked mud all over your floor. We came through quite a rain on the way here."

"No bother, Miss. Enjoy your stay. If ye need anything, jus' le' me know. Alfie'll find it for ye. The girls' dorm is down the hall and to yer left; kitchen and showers straight ahead."

Paula found an empty bunk and lay out all her wet clothes and bedroll to dry. Luckily the beds were furnished with sheets and blankets unlike many of the other hostels she frequented. Her source for a great place to stay was, indeed, very reliable. Hot water was next in her sights. She soon stood in the shower soaking in the heat, hoping to reach room temperature before all the hot water was gone.

* * * * *

Her rides the last couple of days were curious. Paula toured Dublin for three days where her most interesting encounter was with two young schoolgirls from Belfast. They ogled her in the shower because she had "stripes" and wanted to know if these felt the same as her "real skin." Actually they were prominent tan lines garnered from a beach in Portugal. She realized how bronzed she did appear compared to the local fair-skinned population and how unusual for an English-speaker that must seem. Her peculiar appearance also attracted the attention of a little boy who ran up behind her and pulled her long hair to see if it was real.

Paula left Dublin bound for Cork in a beat up second-hand once-luxury hearse, converted to a sleeping van of sorts by the two college boys who drove it. They were headed for the coast on holiday and fixed up their vehicle for eating and sleeping and just about anything else, since they were traveling on a pretty tight budget. When they found out their hitchhiker was American, they asked if she knew the Kennedy brothers, Jack and Bobby. She answered that no, regretfully she did not know them personally; America was a big country. But she voted for Bobby in the California election and had the privilege of shaking Jack's hand at a campaign rally when he was running for president. At that, their faces became doleful and their speech choked as they recounted the esteem in which the two brothers were held in Ireland and at the fateful turn of events which cut both of their lives so short. "We thought of them as brothers. Jack came for a visit in '63, ye know. And many houses display his photo in a prominent place along with the Pope's."

Thus the conversation continued with all the "what ifs" and "might have beens." Despite their more than appealing invitation as they approached Cork, Paula begged off spending the night with the boys in their hearse; she was not on that tight a budget! Instead she thanked them for the ride, hefted her pack onto her back and left their company.

The following day her rides to Limerick were unremarkable except for the length of time she had to wait between them. There were lots of folks who were going "just to the next village" and were most willing to take her that far, so she made slow but steady progress. The hearse boys told her about a great hostel on the western coast, Valentia Island in County Kerry, so after a few hours in Limerick, she was anxious to be on her way west. She caught a lift with an older couple who claimed to be going that way. When they let her out at a junction in the middle of nowhere, they told her it was just down that road a ways. "A ways" turned out to be at least an hour and a half according to the road marker, and the traffic appeared to be infrequent. Oh, well. Paula knew there would be a hot shower at the end of it, so she plodded down the lonely road. And then it started to rain.

Yes, the sports car rescue probably ranked a close second to the hearse.

* * * * *

Paula pulled on her least damp dirty clothes, twisted her wet hair up and fixed it with a clip, and grabbed her most presentable sweater. Then she headed out for food. When she stopped to inquire at the desk where she might find a hearty meal, Alfie handed her a postcard—of the island. Puzzled, she turned it over and read the scrawl,

> Dinner
> 7:30
> T.

If that were an invitation, it seemed rather abrupt. She considered other rides that turned into meals and what that implied, particularly in France and Italy. After her first escape across a freeway from an invitation to a meal that expected her as the dessert course, she vowed never to combine the two again, at least not when she traveled alone. Safety first. But this offer was so perfunctory, it was intriguing. There was undoubtedly more security in a public place in a crowded village where her presumable host was obviously well known than there was in the cab of a long haul truck, she reasoned. She checked the clock.

"Alfie?" she asked. "Where could I go for a nice hot meal?"

"Would ye not be waitin,' Miss? Mr. Thomas'll be along soon to fetch ye." She glared at him until his face turned a rosy blush as he tried to recover his dignity. "No harm meant, Miss Paula. 'E was real insistent I should give ye this card before ye slipped away, so I been aholdin' it right 'ere in me hand right in front o' me so's I wouldna forget."

"Well then, could you recommend some place in case he falls asleep and is too late... or he forgets... or I want to go out for breakfast in the morning instead of fixing something here?"

"Ooh, that won't be necessary, Miss. If 'e says 'e'll be here, then 'e'll be here. Mr. Thomas is a man of his word."

"What time do you lock up here at night?"

"Eleven o'clock, Miss. But no worries. Ye just come anytime ye want and knock at the second window 'round the corner to the right. Alfie'll let ye in."

Great, she thought. My reputation is already in question and I have not even been here a day!

Resigned to her fate, Paula settled into a chair to wait. She thought to herself, standard wait-time for a professor is ten minutes. A stranger is certainly not due more than that, even if he is kind. Then she let her eyes close, just for a minute, to rest. It had already been a very long day.

When Paula opened her eyes, there was a man sitting opposite her, leaning forward with elbows on knees, hands clasped, just staring at her. His dancing (blue, she now noticed) eyes gave Tom away, but his cleanly shaven face and freshly pressed clothes were a surprise to her. The scruffiness disappeared and was replaced with a very pleasing mien.

"You clean up well," she said.

"As do you. I trust you haven't run the whole village dry of hot water."

"I don't think so. But I am still damp all the way through."

"Let's get some hot food into you, then." He pulled her up from the chair and guided her out the door and down the road toward the village.

Paula observed that Tom was a bit taller than she was, but not long and lanky by any stretch of the imagination; stocky was a better description. His bearing was proud but not haughty—confident. He was not "to die for handsome" like Paul Newman, but the strength of his features portended distinction in later life. He had a typically Irish ruddy complexion and broad face. His wavy hair mostly behaved. He did not appear sullen exactly, but the intermittent liveliness in his slate blue eyes did not overshadow his solemn demeanor. He was definitely in command and assumed the lead in their partnering naturally.

Tom did not think Paula was drop-dead gorgeous, but she was striking—slender, tawny and well proportioned. Her hair was the color of rich dark chocolate. He wished he could see it down; he was partial to silky hair with a hint of curl. She had a tall forehead and deep green eyes which gave way to prominent cheekbones and a strong jaw—a very distinctive look, unlike most of the girls he knew. She was self-assured without pretending any air as she moved easily beside him and matched his stride. He was most taken with her broad engaging smile; if she were Irish, he would say there was "blarney" in that smile. He wished he could share her apparent ease with the unpredictable.

Their eatery that evening seemed to be the only one in the village other than the two pubs they passed. As soon as they entered the cozy establishment and worked their way past the bar, an older man greeted them. "Good evenin' Mr. Thomas. We heard ye was in town. Nice to see ye again. How's the Auntie?"

"Still her feisty old self, sharp-tongued as ever. Donald, I'd like you to meet my American friend, Miss Paula. She's traveling through Ireland and heard that Valentia Island was *the* place to find good food and friendly folk." Turning to his guest, Tom continued, "Donald here is about the friendliest folk around and head of this fine establishment. We've come for our supper, Donald."

"Pleasure to meet ye, Miss." And then with a wink to Tom, "I heard ye weren't comin' alone. We've got some mighty good Scampi this evenin' and yer table's ready. I'll bring ye out the usual right away."

"You're a good man. Much obliged."

The restaurant itself was narrow, built like a pier out to the water and then later enclosed. It was not much better than two tables wide. The tables themselves were wooden, mismatched and marred from years of use. Hand-tatted off-white mats in the center of each held the décor together beneath soft yellow light from old oil lamps. Tom led Paula to the one at the front near the window overlooking the harbor. This table remained empty even though most of the others were occupied. It had, no doubt, been saved for him.

As he pulled a chair out for her, it scraped across the uneven planked floor. When she was settled, he seated himself across the table from her in a chair without a mate whose protests at being moved were equally grating. First opening doors, proper introductions, and now pulling out her chair displayed a very gentlemanly manner, Paula thought. Tom orchestrated the evening thus far without consulting her, but it came so naturally and seemed so right. He no doubt had an exemplary model, perhaps his father.

Paula was embarrassed to admit she had no idea what Scampi was. She was so hungry she felt it could not be any worse than the squid stuffed with squid she consumed on the boat coming over, and she survived that well enough. Donald brought their sudsy lager. Hers was the accepted half-pint for women. She took a sip expecting it to be room temperature… and it was. She, like most Americans, preferred her stout cold, but this would do just fine as long as it did not go to her head too quickly.

Since Tom seemed a bit subdued, Paula began the conversation. "I was surprised to get your invitation out tonight. Wasn't your Aunt expecting you to stay and visit?"

"Ordinarily she would. But this being her 'supper and cards night,' my choice was between trying to get a word in edgewise with four old women nattering away or taking my chances with a mysterious stranger. I thought you'd be the better bargain," he explained.

"I hope I won't disappoint."

Before he could reply, Donald brought their dinner and another round. Tom raised his glass. "I forgot to ask your favorite brew."

"Cider."

"Well, we'll have to do something about that now, won't we," he stated with a quirky smile. "This foamy black ale is the drink of choice around here."

"And my limit is one per night," Paula added, glancing at her second half-pint.

"We'll have to do something about that too."

The Scampi was a delight: shelled fleshy tail meat from the Dublin Bay prawn, ale-battered and deep-fried. Boiled potatoes smothered in butter and peas completed the plate. Paula tried not to wolf down her food. She did not want to seem a glutton, but she sopped up every last bit of sauce with brown bread and washed it all down with her second half-pint, which now tasted very good.

During the meal, their conversation was like playing the childhood game of "Categories." They took turns selecting the category. For the most part, their responses erupted almost in tandem.

Major field of study.

P: Liberal Arts curriculum with a Social Anthropology major

T: Classical curriculum with a Business major

Favorite class.

P: Sociology of War and Conflict

T: Establishment of the Irish Free State

Most boring class.

P: Econ, without a doubt

T: Econ was the worst!

Artist.

P: Monet and the way he played with changing sunlight

T: John Constable's landscapes

P: Winslow Homer—man and the sea

T: Joseph Turner—man and the elements, particularly the sea

Paula took a few seconds to try to veer away from the natural.

P: Marc Chagall's flights of fancy

Tom countered with Michelangelo's Sistine Chapel.

Paula had to agree he won that round.

Composer.

Paula did not think it fair to suggest George Gershwin or Aaron Copland. They were too "American," so she proffered Stravinsky instead.

T: Lord, no! He's too unconventional. It has to be Mozart!

Paula's laugh at the unrestrained outburst caused Tom to regain his control.

Music.
P: Musical comedy. I know all the lyrics.
T: Opera. It is more refined and complex.

Band.
P: The Beatles and their new *Sgt. Pepper* album
T: The Rolling Stones, when I can get a hand on their records. Censorship, you know.

Singers.
P: I never liked Elvis much, but I cried when Buddy Holly's plane went down. I'll go with folk singers Bob Dylan, Joan Baez and the group Peter, Paul & Mary.
T: Any Irish tenor who brings simplicity and purity to traditional Irish ballads.
Paula found his sentiment touching.

20th Century Authors.
P: Steinbeck
T: Banned
P: Hemingway
T: Banned
P: J.D. Salinger
T: Banned
P: Ayn Rand?
T: Never heard of him/her, so could be banned. I don't know.
In frustration Paula tried Irishman James Joyce.
T: Banned, but I have read his *Portrait of the Artist as a Young Man* on the sly.
P: *The Dubliners*, in Lit class. I started *Ulysses*, but I'm sorry to say I didn't get far.
T: Likewise… and likewise.

Playwrights.
Finally they found an area of agreement. George Bernard Shaw: He liked *Pygmalion*; she liked *St. Joan*; Samuel Beckett: *Waiting for Godot* was the greatest! And there was no dispute about Shakespeare.

"How is it you know your banned playwrights but not your authors?" Paula asked.

"It's easier to step out for an evening of theater in London than it is to buy a book and get it read before a plane lands in Dublin. I rather like knowing how a story ends."

Favorite character from Shakespeare.
P: Portia.   She was a woman of strength, intelligence and cleverness.
T: King Richard III who was ruthless and defiant but brave to the end.
Both Paula's eyebrows arched up in disbelief.
"Conscience is but a word that cowards use," Tom quoted dramatically. "Act V, Scene III. I know it well. I played Richard in school once. He sought not to be guided by guilt as so many of us raised in the Church today are," Tom explained. He shifted from ease to restraint as he listened to his own words.

Paula tried to lighten the mood a bit.
Favorite after-work activity.
P: Coffeehouse with friends
T: Pub with the fellows

Favorite getaway activity.
P: Hiking in the mountains
T: Sailing the Irish Sea

Favorite getaway destination.
P: Paris, absolutely!
T: Right here on Valentia?
P: Doesn't count.
T: Puffin Island.
Paula screwed up her face and asked, "Where's that?"
T: Not far.

Poet.
P: Walt Whitman—his idea that one is a part of, and an equal to, every man
T: Thomas Moore—our deeds cannot escape the All-knowing
P: W.B. Yeats—be careful when giving your heart
T: W.B.Yeats—the heart once given, be careful your dreams are not trod upon

They both paused in contemplation. It was obvious to each of them that they had very little in common other than a few touch-points, including poetry. Despite their individual ranges of interest being broad and varied, their conversation continued lively and amiable. Tom reflected that an Irish girl would not talk about ordinary things such as they had. Paula was forewarned to eschew the incendiary topics of politics, religion and sex; the Irish would never discuss them with strangers. He, however, seemed determined to tackle every one.

Politics?

P: Registered Democrat who is more a liberal independent

T: Conservative who can't declare a party because of the neutrality required in the news business

Religion?

P: Baptized Methodist; currently more a spiritualist

T: Irish Catholic, cradle to grave and all phases in between

Sex?

Paula's first impulse was to blurt out, "Yes, please." But she quickly covered her mouth to stifle the words and a smile as her cheeks pinked beneath her tan.

Tom felt a deep flush rising from his chest up his throat to his face, past his brows to his hairline. He was surprised he said such a thing to a girl. He was just as surprised she did not seem insulted by his inappropriateness. He tried to recover. "Young adult male with not enough sense, obviously, to know when to keep his impure thoughts to himself." Then, in an effort to make up for his social *faux pas*, his ease became measured restraint once again and the playfulness of the moment was lost.

"What makes a girl set her sights on four years of college?" Tom asked seriously.

"It never occurred to me that I was born the wrong sex, that I was a girl with limited choices: housewife, nurse, secretary or teacher," Paula began. "I was brought up believing I could be anything. One week I wanted to write stories; another, to write plays. I would design houses on graph paper. I wanted to be a dancer, inventor, doctor and attorney for the poor. I wanted to drive a fire engine, run a tractor, raise horses, explore China, illustrate books, design clothes and fly airplanes, not all at the same time of course."

As she continued her discourse, he seemed to relax again. "There was nothing out of my reach. I always knew I would go to college and would need a scholarship to do so. 'What are you going to be when you grow up?' my father would ask. If I said 'a writer,' he would say, 'Oh, that will only take about four years of college.' If I said 'architect,' he would say, 'That might take as many as four years of college.' Driving a tractor or fire engine would also require 'four years of college,' according to my father."

Tom chuckled at the cleverness of her father's trickery and settled back in his chair to enjoy the rest of the story.

"In my early teens, my father added, 'You'll need a scholarship for four years of college to do that' every time we had the profession conversation. By the time I was in high school, I understood I had the freedom to pursue anything I wanted. All it would take was a scholarship for four years of college, and that was up to me to earn. Marriage and motherhood were never part of the conversation—unlike for so many of my school friends." Paula noticed Tom stiffen with her last remark.

He leaned forward to take his turn. "I always knew I was meant to go into the family business. We are not 'old' money, that is to say 'landed for generations.' We're considered 'new' money from commerce. The extended family had small farms in the west but not extensive properties. When I was nine, my father asked me in front of guests at a garden party what I was going to be when I grew up. With a big grin, I answered 'a farmer.' My father turned an irate red and banished me from the gathering. My mother, always the mediator, came to calm me. She reminded me that I wasn't asked what I *wanted* to do. I was asked what I was *going* to do, and that would be 'follow in the business.' No argument. The family worked long and hard at great sacrifice to leave the farms of the west behind, so I wasn't to entertain any fanciful ideas of doing other than my duty to the family.

"Interestingly," Tom continued, "my sisters were never asked. They understood they would marry and bear children. That's why summers here on Valentia seemed so sacred, I suppose. They were a chance for me to be a free spirit, a chance to follow passions I knew I wouldn't be able to in future. So, there was never any question I would go to university and major in business. I was destined to follow the family's path, and I would marry and raise sons who would do the same."

Paula was shocked at the lack of choice Tom's privileged life allowed him. She understood better his efforts to control his manner.

Donald appeared to clear away the plates and to ask if they cared for any "afters." Tom declined—for both of them. He turned their attention toward the harbor and pointed out various types of fishing boats and sailing vessels, the prominent clock tower, and the lighthouse standing guard over all. He listed the many species of fish that were found in nearby waters: conger eel, halibut, turbot, brill, red sea bream and dogfish. Halibut was the only fish Paula recognized and hoped it would be a choice on any menu she might encounter; the others sounded positively scary. Then he rose, signaling the end of the meal. This time when he came around the table to pull out her chair, she was expecting him.

No ticket was brought to them; Tom just left a stack of bills on the bar as he nodded good night. The help nodded back in appreciation, knowing there would be pints for all after closing. Paula thought a polite smile from her would be appropriate, and she was amazed at how their gestures conveyed more meaning than words.

* * * * *

A mossy scent after the day's rain still lingered in the air as they left. "Now, I've been thinking we should take a tour of the village and tell you its truths and its tales. What do you say?" Tom asked as he pointed Paula down a gravel road along the western side of the village.

"That would be great," she replied. "I'd love to know how an Irish island got a Spanish name. My freighter docked in Valencia, Spain, for a couple of days where I saw some good Flamenco, ate oranges and marveled at the El Greco skies every night. I'm looking for a connection between the two. Is there one?"

"Who knows?" he answered. "Maybe the Spanish traders who sailed into our harbor and saw our rainy, rocky little island wished they were back home in Valencia eating oranges and dancing, so for spite they gave it the name of their home port but threw a 't' in there. In case they were asked to sail to Valen*t*ia again they would know a ship was headed north and could decline. Today some maps show it one way, some the other."

Tom enjoyed sharing the island's history as they walked, his companion assuming the role of audience happily. "The island isn't very big as islands go, only about... give me a minute to convert... only about seven miles long by two miles wide, and not many live here, maybe 700 at most. When the quarry was operating back to the northeast, there were more. It was mined for slate in the 1800's and it's said that our slate was used to roof the British House of Commons. Most folks nowadays depend on fishing for their livelihood. Or agriculture. If your potatoes tasted a little suspect, that was probably due to the seaweed fertilizer commonly used.

"The knight of Kerry established this village, Knightstown, in the mid-1800's and not long after, the first transatlantic cable was laid from New York right to here. The cable station gave men work too, but it's been closed for some time." Tom slowed and began looking closely at the bushes lining the road. "Along here a little further, I think we can find an ogham stone... just there. It will be hard to see in the dark, but maybe you can feel the inscription on it." They bent down in front of an oblong stone standing upright. Paula ran her hand from top to bottom and felt a long indentation with notches and hash marks in various groups and at varying angles marked through the vertical. "The characters are ancient Irish," he said. "I don't know what the inscription says. Maybe, 'No oranges on this island.' "

She chuckled at the improbability of it.

Tom's demeanor relaxed again and the cadence of his speech slipped easily into that of the villagers as he resumed his story. "On down this way is a souterrain we used to play in as kids. Just there, all covered over with brambles. I'm not sure we can see in anymore, nor wriggle in for that matter. On a hot day—and you can guess there weren't many of those—being in such an underground chamber felt so cool and refreshing, some of the village boys and I spent hours inside imagining ourselves hiding out from Spanish pirates or ferocious monsters until someone came looking for us. Our excursions down under ended when I carried home the carcass of a fox I found way at the back. I thought it was quite a treasure, but Aunt Moira didn't feel the same. I wouldn't recommend this as a playground these days. Who knows what varmints or reptiles holed up here? We didn't ever consider there might be dangers then; we were just looking for a good time."

He gestured to the left. "Let's turn down this path here and pass by the church." As they walked through the south end of the village, they stopped frequently to examine some point of interest or other which recalled to him the antics of his boyhood. Tom was, apparently, quite a scamp in his youth, Paula gathered, and wondered what changed him. He seemed so tightly strung when they first met. She watched with interest as his mood shifted from ease to restraint throughout the evening.

A bronzed plate, fixed to the front of a modest grey stone building, proclaimed it as the village church. They climbed over the rock wall into the back of its property and crept across its well-tended gardens. Tom's eyes grew wide and his voice became animated as he recounted further tales of mischief and misadventure. Apparently there were many. "Have a look down this Holy Well, won't you?" He dropped a coin and waited for its plunk to indicate depth. "Its waters are said to cure ailments such as warts, toothache and foot pain. Care for a drink?" he offered. She declined graciously.

They continued walking east to the other side of the village, Tom with his hands in his pockets talking on about the surroundings and obviously enjoying his role as guide. He seemed more relaxed and at ease when he told her about his boyhood summers. Paula was content being a good listener. He said that for him, coming to the island was a step back in time to more carefree days. With his job and his family responsibilities now he appreciated that memory.

The couple arrived at what Tom termed the Altazamuth Stone, so called because of the instrument used to determine lines of longitude and by extension the size of the world. Two such markers were placed, again in the mid 1800's: one on Valentia Island and the other in the Ural Mountains of Russia. He explained that proper instrumentation for determining longitude was important to shipping because vessels couldn't navigate safely without knowing where the shorelines actually were. Lives and precious cargo were lost as ships ran into rocky shores thinking they were further out in the ocean.

Paula remarked that there seemed to be a lot going on in the 19th century. What happened in the 20th? He replied smartly, "Well, we finally got electricity a few years ago!"

They turned north continuing at a casual pace and ended near the ferry landing. Paula asked how late the ferry ran.

"Oh, last run is about 15 minutes after the pubs close. Not many come over from the mainland in the evening, so it's rarely someone gets left on the island for the night. You might notice there are a couple of skiffs pulled up on each side of the channel and some cars are parked over at Reenard Point. If a fellow gets left, he can row himself across to his car and just leave the skiff on the other side. The ferry will tow it back the next morning. Remember, it's only about half a mile across. That's how I made it to the island in summer. I'd borrow one of the skiffs and row it back to find our adventures with my village friends. The relations reckoned that when I was strong enough to row across, then I was probably grown enough to be on my own. Besides, the ferryman was always around to fish me out of the water if need be," he rambled on.

"Truth or tale?"

"Mostly truth," Tom grinned.

"And what if you get stranded with your car on *this* side?"

"That's why not many bring their cars over. If a fellow does get stranded, he has to hope that once he's rowed himself across he'll find a car left with keys in it or a bicycle that he can use to get home. Or he can always just sleep in his own car here 'til morning and hope he can make it home before the wife and kids awaken to find him still gone."

"That is one tall tale," Paula accused.

Tom's eyes twinkled and he continued. "They say they'll be building a bridge soon from Portmagee down south. It will surely make the trip more convenient, but a ferry gives one pondering time and maintains the slow pace here which is one of the beauties of life on an island."

"I take it you have firsthand experience with getting yourself home after hours," she teased, glad that his attitude lightened up again.

"It only takes once to learn that you better be watching your time in the evening!"

"Then we better be heading back so you aren't faced with having to decide between car and skiff. Your sleek two-seater is very nice but it's definitely not comfortable enough for an all-nighter," Paula joked.

Tom laughed at her suggestion. "I'll be fine. No worries."

He was decidedly not the merry Irishman Paula heard about, but she was beginning to detect an amiable young man fighting against his guarded formality.

Their conversation finally ebbed. Tom felt invigorated enough to go on, but he could tell Paula was feeling the exhaustion of her day, so he reluctantly guided her back to the hostel. She started to thank him again for the rescue and now for the meal, tour and conversation when he took her hand in both of his and held it for several seconds.

"No," he said. "No further thanks are necessary. It has indeed been my pleasure. I've enjoyed every minute I've spent in your company today—even the wet ones." And with that, in a very gentlemanly manner, like an episode from a Victorian romance novel she thought, he raised her hand to his lips and kissed it tenderly. Then he walked down the steps of the hostel's porch, jumped into his car and sped away.

As tired as she was, Paula took the time to evaluate her evening and her partner in conversation. The meal was superb, their converse intellectually stimulating if not revealing, and Tom ranked somewhere between the nuclear engineer and Britain's former Ambassador to Chile in manner and charm. She looked forward to other rides being so congenial.

Chapter 3

Paula awoke the next morning to the soggy reality of her belongings. Her clothes, only partially dry, were a muddy mess and her bedding was nowhere near ready to be rolled and used again anytime soon. She accepted reluctantly that she would not be leaving the island that day. Luck o' the Irish, the hostel boasted a washing machine! No drier though. No matter. While the clothes were washing, she could stretch cord for a clothes line along and between the bunks and open out her bedroll over a chair in front of the... oh, my goodness... *sunny* window!

She took stock. Everything needed washing and she should take the opportunity to do it while she could. No telling when she would have such extravagant facilities again. But she would have to wear something, the least abused if there were such. She donned her mini-skirt, a top shrunk beyond all modesty in the previous wash and her cleanest over-blouse (missing only one button). Undergarments? ...All but one; the over-blouse should provide adequate camouflage above. Shoes? Into the wash; sandals on feet. Kerchief? Into the wash; hair in a single plait down her back. Towel and swimsuit? Into the wash.

While her laundry churned away, Paula updated her journal and adjusted her itinerary. She could not leave for Galway until the next day and that would push back her arrival in Donegal until midweek; Belfast by the weekend. After a trudge through Scotland, she should still be able to make the concert at Woburn. When all was washed and hung to dry, she set out to find nourishment, to discover what she missed in the walk about the village the previous night, and to find a sunny spot where she would feel free to linger with her thoughts.

She chose the village's one bakery for her breakfast. She entered to, "Mornin.' Ye must be Mr. Thomas' friend Miss Paula. How are ye likin' our island?"

"Very much. But I think I need to examine it more closely in the daylight to get a better feeling for what a nice place you have here. It came highly recommended by other travelers, so I'm really glad I came. I think I'll just take this with me to enjoy while I go exploring."

The proprietress handed Paula four rolls wrapped in a napkin and a hot mug of tea. When she started to protest, the woman said merrily, "Ye can't have a proper cup o' tea in a paper cup, now, can ye? When yer finished, just set it down on any windowsill and it will come back to me. They always do. Enjoy your stay, then."

She nodded a smile and left with the mug of tea and rolls enough for two days, amazed at how invisible her movements and activities were *not*.

* * * * *

Tom found Paula that afternoon south of the harbor on the only clean slip of grass there. Her eyes were closed. She might be sleeping; musing, more likely. He studied her for a long time. What he took as robustness yesterday, piled in all those clothes, today was revealed as slender and curvaceous. She could have been in short shorts for all her mini-skirt covered, and her skin-tight top left very little to the imagination. Her limbs were long and lanky but did not seem out of proportion to her body, enhanced as they were by a healthy musculature and a deep shade of bronze. Her feet were bare, showing stripes where her sandals had been on some other sunny day. Her dark hair was in a thick braid, which curled around her neck and over her shoulder. Her head rested on a rumple that could be a shirt or wrap of some kind. He thought of the girls he knew, the women in his family who were fair or rosy, red-headed for the most part, some petite, some plump, but none so comely in her way, and he wondered how this enchanting foreigner wandered into his life.

He finally approached and stood over her. "You seem to have brought the only sunny day to Ireland yet this year." When Paula started at his voice, he added, "May I join you?"

She nodded in the affirmative, brought herself to a sit and patted the grass beside her, shading her eyes with the other hand. "I'm just biding my time while my clothes dry. It's been laundry for me today," she said. "I'm thankful for the warmth of the sun. Even my sweaters needed airing."

"What have you done with your day besides wash clothes and soak up sun?" Tom sat, but not too close, and was disappointed when she put on her blouse and tied its tails around her waist.

"I took a daylight tour, retracing our route from last night. I found the ogham stone again and took a rubbing of its inscription." She removed a paper from her skirt pocket and flattened it against the ground. "You'll see there are no repeat notching patterns, so it couldn't say 'No oranges;' there are not two O's in succession. And the stones predate the Spaniards by several centuries. You have been caught telling a tale," she kidded.

A crinkle of a smile escaped Tom's lips. "I confess."

Paula refolded the paper and returned it to her pocket. "The entry to the souterrain is blocked with stones. Cautious parents probably thought that was a good idea after hearing reports of *your* misadventures. Apparently there are some really ancient stone beehive huts down at the south end of the island, presumably used by monks following St. Patrick." She took note of the slight disbelief on Tom's face and explained, "I ran into some village folk who were happy to share tales too.

"I walked over to the ferry dock and timed its run so I'll know how to plan when I leave tomorrow," Paula continued. "I gather the schedule is 'flexible' and 'on demand.' It takes only about five to seven minutes to cross, but the loading and unloading of cars takes that much more so one crossing really takes about a quarter of an hour. Or if I just miss it, I'll have at least a thirty-minute wait. I guess a person must plan for a lot of 'pondering time' as you said. Then I walked past the harbor and looked at the fishing boats again. Not many were still in by the time I got there, so I wandered down here to find something softer than stone to lie on while the sun was still out.

"How about you?" She turned toward Tom and flashed a fetching smile. "What brings you over to the island today? I thought you came all this way to visit with your aunt."

He looked straight into her deep green eyes and answered, "You," then glanced away, "…and I did. I've just barely escaped her probing into my life."

"Tell me about her. Is your aunt your mother's sister or your father's?"

"Neither, actually." Tom launched into his history. "I have this thick Irish Catholic blood running through my veins on both sides, and my family has more branches than an old oak tree. The O'Connells have been in County Kerry forever. My mum was a Fitzgerald from around Cork. Aunt Moira is really Mum's youngest aunt, the rebel in her family who married an Ahearn. The Fitzgeralds and the Ahearns didn't get along, so Uncle Daniel and Aunt Moira moved out to the west coast to get away from all the brouhaha surrounding the two feuding families.

"My mother and father met on one of Mum's many visits to her aunt, and since the O'Connells and the Fitzgeralds were *not* on the outs at the time, they were able to marry and move to Dublin. My father went into business there with an assortment of uncles, brothers and cousins who had already moved east. Business stays in the family, as I've said. Summers, my sisters divided their time between Cork and County Kerry, but I always liked staying with Aunt Moira best. She followed society's rules and knew her place as wife and mother, but she understood boys and their longings… although she was never too keen on my souterrain adventures," he added.

He began to pick blades of the long sea grass and split them down center, smiling as he continued. "I may be the head of my family now, but Aunt Moira still sees me as a mischievous boy, up to no good as likely as not, who needs to be put in his place now and again... and she thinks she's the best one to do that. I humor her by coming three or four times a year just so she can."

"And has she? Put you in your place this trip?"

Tom stopped and nodded his assent. "Absolutely. Why do you think it took me so long to get here this afternoon? She shook her finger at me all morning telling me how she knew I'd shown up with a girl this trip and I'd better be minding my manners and not compromising the family name. (*Which* family name, she didn't say.) She wanted to make sure you weren't a shirttail Ahearn or a Dempsey in disguise, as she didn't want to revisit the brouhaha days. That was too hard on everybody, she now admits. She reminded me that I'm not yet thirty so I shouldn't even be looking at girls, let alone traveling with one. I've got my sisters to look after—one who is getting married in a couple months' time—and what did I know about her 'young man' as she calls him."

Noting her interest, he resumed. "That took the conversation away from me and on to the rest of the family, thank goodness. After I helped her muck out the garden shed, she decided I'd suffered enough at her hand and gave me my freedom for what remained of the afternoon and evening." He paused and stared out to sea. "As I left, she gave me a pat on the shoulder and said, 'Remember, Thomas. You must be strong enough to accept a little private sin in your life, and then let it go and move on.' "

"What did she mean?" Paula asked, weaving his discard grasses.

He turned toward her again. "I don't know. We Irish are the masters of sin and guilt. I've probably sinned at least five times on the way here just by hoping you hadn't already disappeared down the road before I could free myself from my aunt." He averted her gaze. "Speaking of sin... how do you manage, traveling alone?"

Paula was a little taken aback. "Are you suggesting that riding in cars alone with strangers is sinful?"

Tom drew up his hands in defense and responded quickly. "No! Not at all! Getting a lift in rural Ireland is a way of life for villagers who all know one another. But young Irish girls would never climb into a car with a stranger at the risk of a reputation or worse. You being a foreigner... I was thinking that a lot of men who would stop to pick up a strange girl might have lechery on their minds; that you might find yourself in rather compromising situations sometimes. That's all."

"And did *you*? Have lechery on *your* mind when you stopped for me?"

"No! Not at all! I mean… not that I wouldn't want to…. You're awfully…. But… This isn't going very well, is it?" Plum-faced, he shook his head.

"Nope. I think you've got yourself into a corner," she agreed.

"Let me try again." Tom chose his words carefully. "I should think it would be dangerous for anyone, but especially for a woman, to travel alone and be so dependent on strangers, never being sure just what their intentions were in picking her up. Is it not dangerous?"

Paula chuckled at his feeble attempt to recoup. "Yes, it can be dangerous, but no more so than sharing a compartment on a train with *five* strangers who may have more than travel on their minds. I refuse rides when I get the wrong vibes from a glint in the eye or a crooked smile. I've also learned some tricks that work pretty well: wielding heavy blunt objects and separating myself from drivers. It's never advisable to accept food from a ride, I've learned. If a man offers, it generally means he has appetite for more than the meal! Most folks are genuinely nice and just want to help, and all of them make up for the few I'd rather forget."

"So, I must not have had that glint in my eye nor a crooked smile that scared you off," he cajoled.

"Frankly, I was so cold and so wet that I didn't even care. Besides, I knew you'd never make it past my pack in your little car."

"Then why did you accept a meal from *me* last night? Do I appear *that* harmless?" he queried with pretend indignation.

"Curiosity, I suppose, that you would *command* me to. There was no question mark on your postcard. Everyone here seemed to know about you and your doings, so I figured you couldn't have anything too clandestine in mind. Besides, I was starving," she admitted.

Tom broke into a full out grin. "Let's dismiss the safety factor, then. What are the advantages of traveling alone? Don't you ever get lonely?"

"Well, I meet more interesting people, for one thing. I'd never have met *you* if I hadn't been alone!" Paula patted his arm, and he welcomed it. "Two people my size wouldn't have fit in your car, for another. Folks are more likely to pick up a single than two or more, so I get rides more quickly. A girl alone seems less threatening to another woman or a family or a group of young kids. A couple usually feels sorry for me, and I'm not above playing that pity card."

Paula turned more serious and shifted to face him. "Drivers going a long distance know they can count on conversation and company. They actually seek something to make the time and the miles pass more quickly. I provide a welcome diversion for them. Enclosed in the front seat of a car or the cab of a truck, folks feel safe to unburden themselves, say whatever they feel. I find out more about a people and how they think, their mores, their values, their challenges and their joys than I ever would by staying in one place for six months. When traveling as a twosome, conversation with the driver doesn't happen. The hitchers usually sit in the back and talk to each other. When one-on-one, the conversation is more fluid, frank and open, as if one's thought had voice."

Tom tried to imagine hitchhiking at all. He knew *he* never would have.

"By staying in hostels, I meet lots of kids from all over the world who are doing the same thing I am," she went on. "Some I pal up with for a few days; others I see over and over again in other towns. There's always someone to talk with if I need company, but when I want to be alone I can be without offending anyone."

Paula looked at him rather intently. "As an individual, one doesn't have to fit a traditional profile. I'm not an American; I'm just me. I try not to conform to any stereotypes of *the American tourist*, and I certainly don't believe that being one entitles me to any special treatment as many of my fellow travelers do." She stared seriously at him. "How do you perceive Americans? What do you expect from someone introduced to you as American?"

Tom turned toward her and appeared a little uncomfortable to be sharing such an opinion with a relative stranger. "I really haven't known that many of your countrymen—a few through business, of course—and most of them had a pretty good opinion of themselves. They seemed to know what they wanted and expected to get it. Oh, they were friendly and polite on the outside, but I never felt sincerity from them. I've not met many of our age-group, just out of school in their twenties. But if I had to come up with a few adjectives, I would use…" and he hesitated, "…rude, mouthy, obnoxious, boorish, over-confident and entitled. No offense," he hurried to add.

"And what about American women? What comes to mind there?" She could sense his discomfort.

"Vapid. More concerned with style than substance. Pushy. Flirtatious… and doe-eyed. Again, no offense."

"None taken. So, where do I fit into that picture?"

Tom relaxed as he answered, casting an admiring smile at her. "You don't, thank goodness. That's been the delight of the last twenty-four hours. You are absolutely beyond what I imagined when you first introduced yourself as American."

She arched her eyebrows. "What *did* you imagine?"

"All the things I've seen in the news: Anger. Defiance. Guys in dirty torn jeans and maybe a vest, bare feet or sandals or heavy hiking boots, bandana or headband around the forehead, chains of beads around the neck, long hair, unshaven with dirty hands. A back pack. Maybe a guitar."

Paula's eyes widened as he continued. "The girls I imagine in long patterned or flowered skirts, same footwear, same headgear, more jewelry—ankle bracelets, dangly beaded earrings, lots of beaded necklaces, a leather or woven shoulder bag, no makeup except for a peace sign painted on the cheek, and definitely flowers in long hair."

Tom shrugged his shoulders. "It's sort of a unisex image, I guess, except for the beards. I would also expect a tuned out mellowness due to... you know... smoking marijuana."

"I must have scared you to death," Paula laughed.

"Not frightened. 'Make love, not war' and all that," he went on. "Your appearance didn't conform to my image, and as soon as you put more than two sentences together coherently, I decided you probably hadn't been smoking, at least recently. I think I was more worried about smelling up my car than about all the water you dragged in. No, you didn't seem the typical city girl nor the typical 'Hippie.' "

"My point exactly." Paula accentuated each word with a stab to the grass. "And there are a lot more of me out there trying to buck the preconceptions. If we're supposed to come from such a melting pot, if diversity is in our nature, how can we be characterized?"

"I guess you can't," Tom agreed and faced her with a smirk. "Now, to be fair, you have to try to characterize the Irish."

"Hmmm," she thought. "Merry... Friendly... Poetic dreamers... Loyal... Proper... And, loquacious."

"And which of these fine traits can you attribute to me?" Tom asked, sitting up a little straighter.

Paula eyed him from top to toe. "Friendly—you picked me up and you didn't display any reservations when I threatened to flood your car. Definitely proper—you are more than polite, assume the lead in social situations and treat the villagers with respect. Loyal—I can hear it in your voice when you talk about your family, and you acknowledge long-standing relationships. The villagers speak of *you* with respect." Tom sat even straighter at her good report.

"Merry comes and goes. Sometimes your eyes dance, but not often," she continued. "The poetic dreamer I've not seen yet; he might be hidden somewhere inside of you. And then there's loquacious. At first I thought you were either sullen or a man of few words, but last night they were just rolling off your tongue as if held captive there for too long. You enjoyed reminiscing about this island and I could tell." She tilted her head. "How'd I do?"

"Very perceptive, I'd say."

"But there's more." She studied his eyes before she spoke the next. "If I hadn't met you I would not have been exposed to the brooding, introspective, repressed side of the Irish."

Tom seemed a bit affronted and stiffened. "Really? How's that?"

Paula forged ahead trying to catch his eye again, but he kept his face averted. "Brooding—you have something on your mind. It has to do with your position in your family, I think, and new responsibilities that have fallen to you. Introspective—I find you staring at me frequently and I can tell there's a conversation with yourself going on in your head. Repressed—you are fraught with unresolved emotional issues. You stand with your hands in your pockets, your arms crossed or your hands clasped most of the time, and until now you have stayed with 'safe' topics of discussion."

"Wow. How could you read all that?" Her words stung, but she was right. Tom *was* tied up in knots.

"You say a lot with your silence," she continued cautiously. "You have a very limited opportunity here—just as strangers do when I accept rides with them—to speak freely with no consequence. I would guess you don't express yourself frankly even with people you know well. But our dialog should feel safe for you because you know we'll never see one another again after today. You can tell any tale, express any opinion, question anything you doubt, and no one will ever know. It's like whispering secrets to the sea, except the sea won't respond... and I will, if you ask."

Tom became very serious. "You've set up quite a challenge for me then, haven't you?"

"It's your life, your island, your time. I'm just passing through. Use me as you will."

He sat silently, searching for answers in that undulating sea. No contemporary had ever spoken to him so critically before.

Paula broke the silence. "I apologize if I've offended you by being rude, over-confident or pushy—all those things you dislike in Americans. I never should have presumed with 'But there's more.' We parted on such a friendly note last night. I'd like that to be the memory."

"That's impossible now," Tom said slowly, measuring his words.

* * * * *

Paula took a deep breath and chastised herself for being so forward with such a nice guy. She knew better. One does not behave that way with a gentleman, challenging him directly.

Tom unclasped his hands from around his knees and leaned back on his elbows extending himself with full exposure to the sun. "That's impossible now because... I have to accept your challenge. I have to show you that you're not as smart as you think you are; that underneath all the brooding, introspection and repression there lives a thoughtful, merry, poetic, confident, fun-loving Irishman who wants very much to make you eat your words!"

They found relief in a good laugh together, and he basked in the sun of her smile.

They both lay back on the grass, side by side, a little closer than before. In the daylight now Paula saw Tom barely changed from the previous evening, in contrast to herself. His shirt, a fresh one, was still starched and pinstriped. Today he left the top button open. The sleeves of his pullover were pushed up his forearms instead of pulled clear down to his wrists. His slacks were creased, and he was all in shades of grey and tan to match his serious nature. He was wearing the same penny loafers.

After a time, the two rolled to their sides, facing one another. They locked stares and both started to speak at once. They caught themselves and exchanged smiles instead.

She began the inquisition. "You told me you have a great aunt and a sister who is about to be married. Presumably you have a mother and a father but you're the head of the family. You have numerous uncles and cousins. Tell me about them."

Tom relaxed into what might become a long exposition. "Oh, where to begin? You already know about the O'Connells and the Fitzgeralds. My father died a little over two years ago leaving my mother and his five children. I'm the middle child and only son; therefore, at Father's death I became head of the family.

"My father's older brother is really the head of the Dublin O'Connells, but I'm the head of my immediate family. That makes me guardian to my sisters—their 'big brother' so to speak—and technically to my mother, but she won't admit it. Just like Aunt Moira, Mum still thinks she ought to be telling me how to order my life. Frankly, I'm happy that she does because twenty-five is way too young to take on the responsibility of my family."

He checked Paula's attention level and found her following his words with interest while tracing figure-eights in the grass. He deftly placed an index finger to follow hers around the circuit.

"My delight is my four sisters. Kathryn and Anne are older than I. Elizabeth and Margaret are younger. My sorrow is also my four sisters—I need to marry them all off before I even consider marriage and family for myself. Kathryn being the eldest is already married. Anne is to be wed September 17 in Rome. We'll be going there, of course. Luckily Mum and Kathryn have the preparations in hand, so all I have to do is show up for the festivities and give Anne away with my blessing."

Paula chuckled at the image of serious Tom busying himself with wedding details.

"I had to give my consent too which was a farce, for the man's at least ten years older than I and very well established. I was barely out of University and trying to be all serious and proper, but that's the way it's done. Coming from a family of sisters and no brothers for advice, I had to rely on novels and movies as a model for what I should do and say. Really, Robert should have gone to our uncle to ask, and I personally think that he did, but the girls felt this would do, and as I would have to go through it two more times I might as well get the practice in now. Actually, I think they put me on as a tease, but the deed will be finalized here shortly and that's that," Tom concluded.

"So you all *do* have a sense of humor," Paula remarked.

"Rarely. Usually only when we're all together and I'm the butt of it. The girls think I'm a pushover, so I have to practice saying 'No. I don't think so,' with conviction before they've conned me out of every last shilling."

They laughed at his predicament.

"I'm sorry your father died so young. Was it expected?"

"He wasn't particularly young—his mid-sixties. And he'd had heart trouble for a time. It's Mum I worry about. She's quite a bit younger, and now with two of the girls out of the house and me trying to marry off the other two, I think she'll have some lonely years ahead of her."

"You really *do* have cause to brood, then. Is that usual, to marry off the daughters before the sons?" Paula asked.

"It depends on a family's make up," Tom replied. "With Father gone and me the only son, there's no way I could manage two households—one for my sisters and one for myself with wife and children. And a business too? That's unrealistic, even as brilliant and industrious as I am! Besides I'm not likely to marry until I'm thirty-five anyway, so there's time for it all to work itself out. It could be worse. I could have had seven sisters!"

Paula laughed. "Why thirty-five?" she questioned.

"I come from an established social order. That's how it's done. We should know who we are and what we'll be doing with our lives then. By that age a man is thought to have matured sufficiently and to have established himself in his profession well enough to provide properly for a family."

"And how do *you* feel about that?" Paula could not imagine conforming to an arbitrary age rule.

"Well, I can't feel burdened. That's just how it is. Two days ago I felt the weight of the world on my shoulders what with work and some to-do about a dress. I felt I was being thrust into adulthood too fast, and I just wanted that heavy rain to wash it all away for a while. Right now I feel...very... relaxed." Tom turned again onto his back.

Paula turned onto her back as well and urged him on. "What's so troubling at work?"

"Oh! My uncles! Just because we're family doesn't mean we have to agree. We do on most things, but lately we're at loggerheads. Since I'm the youngster and still learning the communications business, they oversee the commercial side of the station and the hard news. I've been given human interest, documentaries, and public notice as my areas of responsibility, those programs that are prepared in advance so my uncles have a chance to review them and assure they will pass the censors. That's all right by me. I know I've not had the years of experience they have and I must start somewhere, but I'm itching for a chance at some hard news."

Tom lifted his head to see if Paula was still awake. He did not want to bore her with his personal concerns. It really was not done to discuss private details or emotions outside the family/friend circle, so he appreciated having the opportunity to vent some and was surprised at what a relief he felt—liberated, even.

"I'm trying to put together a short piece on Northern Ireland, around Belfast, where demonstrations are protesting discrimination against the Catholic minority there. So far it is a peaceful civil-rights-type movement, but I've watched the aftermath of student discontent on your old campus at Berkeley, at Columbia University, in London, and this May at the Sorbonne. Now with Russian tanks apparently rolling toward the border of Czechoslovakia, there's bound to be big trouble there. All it takes is a spark, it seems, and what began as peaceful demonstration can turn into something very ugly.

"I want to put a hard news team up in Belfast so we'll be on the spot if and when trouble breaks there. I don't want to be dependent on local reporting, which is naturally anti-Catholic, for our information. And a local Catholic team couldn't move freely among the Protestant crowds. My uncles don't see it that way. The issues there have existed for years, they say. My uncles think it's just a continuation of more of the same grievances and there's nothing to fear from peaceful demonstration patterned after that of your Martin Luther King Jr. But I see it as potential for really bad things happening. One wrong step, one miscommunication, one young person hurtling a stone or pulling a trigger in anger, and non-violence turns to violence and people start getting hurt."

Paula was staring intently at Tom now, aware of the seriousness in his tone. He continued.

"My uncles think I'm overreacting because of my 'youth,' that no such grand calamity is on the horizon. I can't decide whether I should send a crew up there to sit it out anyway, just in case, or whether I should go up there on my own indefinitely on some pretense. Maybe I should back off because they might be right in the end and it would just be a waste of employee time and money. Then there's the question of censorship. Anything live we got up there would have to go through meticulous editing to be sure of passing the board of censors."

The mention of censorship again really caught Paula's attention. "I can see why you're feeling so overwhelmed and tense. Dare I say, 'introspective and repressed?' You've got way too much on your mind to be sitting here babbling about ogham stones and fishing boats and ferries."

Tom chuckled. "Actually, the diversion is doing me good. I haven't enjoyed casual conversation in a very long time. Everything I'm involved in at home has to have a point to it. I'm thankful for the opportunity to just be mindless for a while."

"So we're mindless now?" Paula quipped.

"I didn't mean anything by that. It's just so nice to be able to speak my mind without being judged...." Tom sighed. "You know what else would be really nice? To lie here in the sun next to you with my eyes closed and be the listener for a while."

"What kind of a tale would you like me to tell?"

"About you... and your family. Are you so-called 'typical'?"

* * * * *

Paula braced herself for a retelling of her bio. "My family tree is not so prolific as yours. I have very few shirttail relatives who interfere in my life, and the few I do have live several miles away from our home, so their influence is minimal. Most everyone in the family is in education in some way. The grandparents farmed, of course. That's why a family would move out west to Colorado. But aunts, uncles and cousins, even though few, all went into teaching in primary or secondary school. My father is a college professor and my mother is a librarian on campus."

"Your mother works?" Tom seemed surprised.

"She has since my brother and I were in school."

"And your father *allows* it?"

"Of course. Why? Is that unusual?"

"I should say so. I don't know many married women, young or old, who work outside the home. Their place is running the household," Tom decreed.

"Well, *my* mother works," Paula stated proudly. "She had to with two children bound for college at the same time. My brother is three years older than I, about your age. He was in graduate school while I was at Berkeley. I couldn't go out to California or to college at all, if I did not have those scholarships. The salaries of a professor and a librarian don't go very far. We live in a three-bedroom house in a small town with parks, a swimming pool, a local C-league baseball team, one high school and a county fair. We ski, hunt and fish, go camping. There are maybe fifteen churches in our town, most of different denominations. The groups intermix amicably, which you say is not the case here. As I said last night, we happen to be Methodist. I couldn't tell you what most of my friends were." Paula concluded, "I'd say that's pretty typical of small town America, at least west of the Mississippi River."

"Do you have just the one brother, then? Your family has only two children?"

"That's right. 'One for each hand,' as my mother would say."

"Why's that?" Tom queried.

"I guess she thought it was *her* responsibility to get us safely to the other side of the road.

"Politically, my parents are slightly on the liberal side. They're true-blue American but not so patriotic that they are willing to sacrifice their son for a war they don't believe in," Paula asserted. "That's what's causing conflict in the family right now. Because of the draft, my brother is likely to be called up any time. My parents are so opposed to his going to Vietnam, that they are putting everything they have into keeping him in graduate school, hoping that he can maintain his student deferment until the war is over. As you know, that doesn't look to be anytime soon." A seriousness returned to Paula's face.

"Chuck's in the sciences now—biology. But once he receives his graduate degree, about the only thing that will extend his deferral is attending some kind of medical school, maybe dentistry. That's

Plan B—why my parents are saving every penny, and I'm taking some time off before graduate school. Once he's through medical school, if drafted, Chuck would not likely be sent to the front lines. He'd probably practice at one of the big bases or staging areas. Plan C— draft dodging, escaping to Canada—is not an option. My parents would never condone anything illegal." Paula seemed resigned to the path her family had chosen.

"My brother, of course, has a mind of his own and thinks that he ought to be allowed to use it. He's not particularly interested in medicine; frankly, he's not interested in science. With the amount of work that goes into a graduate degree, he'd much rather be studying something of his own choosing. He does not take school as seriously as he should and his grades are dropping. If they sink too far, the deferment is gone and the die is cast. On the one hand I don't blame him for feeling so out of control with his own life."

Paula turned her face toward Tom. "Sound familiar?"

"Uh hmm. 'Out of control with one's life' sounds very familiar, but at least I'm not in mortal danger." Tom reached for Paula's hand, and she let him take it.

"On the other hand, I don't want to see him going off to any war, but this war in particular," Paula continued. "There are so many questions surrounding its validity. When I marched in anti-war demonstrations in San Francisco, invariably there were servicemen among the spectators. It was devastating to see the 'why' in their eyes, and I don't want for my brother's to be one of those vacant faces waiting in vain for a peaceful demonstration to change the world. You and I both see that it will take a shock, a violent shock, maybe many, to bring the establishment around. They believe the protesters and demonstrators will get over it; all those kids will get tired and hungry and go home soon, and the status quo will return." She paused. "We are on the cusp of such change in this world....

"My brother and I have great long discussions by letter. Since he must sit down to put pen to paper and actually think about what he writes, I hope that helps him find clarity and calm amidst all the tension at home. My parents mean well. Most parents do."

Paula again turned and locked her gaze on Tom's tormented eyes. "Your uncles have your best interests at heart too, even though they might not know how to express it in a way you understand."

He gave her hand a long firm squeeze. He was beginning to find a comfortable familiarity with this girl such as he had not felt with a female before. "So you have troubles in your life too. And yet you seem so carefree."

"I'm trying to escape from the same things that haunt everyone right now, trying to find that little scrap of peace that will carry me through whatever is meant to come next. A carefree attitude helps, even when it's hard to summon." Paula closed her eyes and let the sun wash over her, content to lie in silence for a while.

Eventually Tom broke that silence. "Yours sounds like a close family. Let's go back to happier times—when you were a schoolgirl."

"I went to the neighborhood school—about six blocks from home. Most of my friends lived nearby. We collected the group, younger and older, as we walked to school. We walked home for lunch too. And we had two play periods a day—recess."

"I was boarded from an early age, maybe ten. I got to go home on Saturdays. Most of my friends were schoolmates since we lived so closely together. After school, sports, meals and studies, we didn't have much free time," Tom explained.

"My mother made my clothes. I had to wear an outfit two days before I could put it in the laundry. I had one pair of shoes for the whole school year. I wore the previous year's shoes for play; they always pinched so I couldn't run fast."

"I wore a uniform: white shirt and tie, blazer, short pants and knee sox and a cap if I left campus. My sisters went to convent school but did not board," he added.

Paula told how she wanted to play piano when she was little but the family could not afford one. She went to a friend's house to listen to her practice. Paula's parents enrolled her in ballet classes instead, requiring only a tutu and slippers—a manageable expense.

Tom was part of his school's Boys' Choir, of course, and had daily practice during school. They sang during Mass on Sundays. When he went home on Saturdays, he had piano lessons and riding lessons. Dance lessons were held at his house too when he was a little older. Social dance, not ballet. His sisters used him as a partner so they could practice. "Was that ever embarrassing!"

"I liked the structure of ballet; each beat had a position," Paula continued. "That's what I enjoy about folk dancing, too, the structure and repetition—and the social aspect. Anyone can do it and many dances do not require partners. Then Rock came along. We learned all the moves by watching *American Bandstand* on TV after school. Dance became a way to stand out... other than academics or athletics. Now, everyone does his own thing, however he's moved to express himself."

"I like the freedom dance now promises, but there are few places to dance like that here... and no time. Most Saturday night dances are of the 'social' variety—waltz, two-step, and traditional Irish jigs, even in the villages," Tom explained.

"I was the kid who thought she had to be first, be the best. I was embarrassed to tears in school when someone beat me at a timed writing of numbers 1 – 100."

"We were rapped on the knuckles with a ruler if we misbehaved. We were embarrassed into compliance with sarcasm if we didn't know an answer or were even considered uncooperative. Mistreatment was thought to build character; tears were not permitted," Tom remembered soberly.

Paula's school day began with the Pledge of Allegiance to the flag, followed by a Bible reading and a chapter from a book. George Washington's portrait always hung above the clock staring down at the class. Sometimes Abraham Lincoln was there too.

Tom attended daily Mass. Religious training was given at school. Pictures of the Pope and the Virgin Mary were displayed in every home.

"Summers we biked, swam, camped and went to the grandparents' farm. We worked as needed, but we played lots of make-believe too. At home we played Sardines, Hide and Seek, Kick the Can—sometimes with the whole neighborhood, including parents. We could turn a living room into a tent city in a flash and assemble elaborate costumes for a drama. We finger painted with chocolate pudding and created museum masterpieces with our dime store water colors. We jumped rope, roller skated and played board games. Mostly we just went out into the yard and made a mess. Even cleaning up had fun in it."

Tom smiled at the pictures she painted with her words, not sure he could imagine himself in them. His experience was so different. "When I think of play, I remember summers here on Valentia; there was no time for play during school. I learned to row by observation. I sat on the main side of the channel to watch. One day a boat was left on the main side, so I climbed in and floundered myself across, finally finding a rhythm. That's when I met the village boys and made my first friends other than schoolmates or cousins. I talked my way onto a fishing boat where I learned their skills... or attempted to. As you can see by this hook's scar here on my thumb, I wasn't very good at first." He displayed with pride an arc across the entire width of his right thumb pad.

"I talked my way onto a sailboat at fourteen and haven't stopped traveling the water since. School was drudgery, but summers were idyllic. I lived for summers and the freedom they promised. My parents would bring me out to Aunt Moira's at the beginning and pick me up at the end and trusted I wouldn't drown in the meantime. That all ended about the age of sixteen when I was expected to spend summers apprenticing at the station. I guess my sports car and my sailboat are symbols of the adolescent rebellion I was never allowed," he said almost to himself.

Paula watched Tom gradually withdraw. He rubbed the fishhook scar on his thumb with his index finger, no doubt recalling not pain, but the pleasure of more carefree times. She attempted to lighten the mood.

"I have a summer scar too. Actually I have lots of them, but this is one of the best," she said enthusiastically as she pointed to her left ankle. Tom noticed a thin white mark marring her deep tan as it snaked its way from bone to bone around the back of her ankle. He winced at the thought of what must have caused it.

"I lost a battle with barbed wire on Grandpa's farm," she offered in answer to his unasked question. "We kids were told time and again not to fight a barb, to call for help instead, if we ever got snagged... but what kid listens. It's a good thing they found me when they did or I might have damaged the tendon and ended my dancing days!"

"That *would* have been disastrous," he agreed. "I thought only boys did silly things like that."

"Oh, no. Not true. I have several badges of honor from trying to keep up with the boys. I always came home bleeding. My mother was mortified that I would never make suitable beauty pageant material," she laughed. "These two," she proudly presented her knees, "are from roller skating, and this one," extending her right elbow, "is from a stupendous bicycle crash."

"I have one of those, too," Tom offered as he hiked up the arm of his sweater to reveal a severely scarred left elbow. "These," he said pulling up his pant legs to expose both damaged knees, "are from Irish football, and this one," he said fingering a slight blemish below his left eye, "is from a right hook I didn't see coming... from my best mate at school, no less."

They laughed and continued to share war wounds and horror stories, matching one another gouge for gouge and scrape for scrape. She had an arc, too, on the bottom of her big toe, from stepping on a tin coffee can lid. He had one on the top of his head from standing up too suddenly in a cave. Her brother hit her above the ear with his toy dump truck. His sisters pushed him off a stone wall into a woodpile as revealed by several puncture wounds across his lower back. She slid her blouse and shirt off her shoulder to reveal the results of an unsuccessful tree climb.

Tom was embarrassed by displaying body parts so freely and put his clothes to rights. Paula did likewise and said she had a pulverized tailbone for all the times she had fallen on her rear. He challenged, "that doesn't count."

"Well," she huffed. "I have the blue ribbon winner right here," and she pointed under her chin. "I was about eleven. I was getting out of the swimming pool. I had my hands on the edge and was about to heft myself up when a pesky boy dove underneath the water, grabbed my ankles and jerked me down so hard that my chin cracked against the cement. The lifeguard hauled me out of the water and lay me down by the pool. Blood was everywhere, and I was crying. My mother wrapped me in a towel and rushed me to the doctor. I came away with six stitches and a big bandage. Mostly I was humiliated that a boy brought me to tears. My mother told me not to be too angry with him; he didn't know how to show that he liked me. 'He'll be sorry for a very long time,' she said."

Paula leaned her head way back to brandish her prize. Tom reached over and stroked it with his thumb. He had never examined the scarred parts of a woman before. His audacity galled him. He did not know what to say or do next but knew it was his turn.

"I've nothing quite so dramatic to share," he said as his hand found its proper place back in the grass. "Every trip to the island was marked with a wound of some sort. My shins and elbows are testament to my trying to find easy access by climbing its rock faces. Salt water washed most of them out so they healed fast. By the end of summer they were barely visible. I may not be able to match you in drama, but I warrant I have surpassed you in number," he said proudly.

"Why climb rock faces when all you had to do was put in at the docks?"

"Oh, I didn't do that here. I was trying to scale Puffin Island."

Chapter 4

They lay back again to soak in the sun and relax in deep thought. "I gather you're not too keen on reliving your recent past," Tom intruded, "but I really would like to know about your days at Berkeley and in San Francisco, an up close and personal account of 'the movement' so to speak. I don't know anyone who has been that near the action, and I'd really like to pick your brain for a different perspective than the one we're fed here."

"Background material for another documentary?"

"Maybe," he admitted. "Really, I'm just interested, but if you'd rather not because it's too personal I'll understand. I'll be disappointed with such a charming opportunity lying right here beside me, but I'll understand."

"Only if you'll reveal some more gory details from your side first," Paula bargained.

"That sounds ominous. What did you have in mind?"

"I'm really interested in your business. If you work in television news, in the dissemination of information, where does a board of censors fit in, and what's with banning authors?"

"Thank you for bringing up another testy issue that I'm wrestling with right now!" Tom stated firmly, "I don't agree with what's done, but I have no choice. It's the law."

Surprised at his reaction, she apologized. "Sorry I hit a nerve. Never mind. I'll back off."

"No. It's only fair. I'll trade you censorship for San Francisco, and I'll go first." Tom sat up in front of her with his legs crossed.

"Originally the O'Connells were in publishing, one of the dailies and a couple of the regionals. That's what took the uncles and then my father to Dublin. The next thing they acquired was the radio station. Then when television came along they were poised to invest there too. The government had control of our radio-television network in terms of policy, but there was plenty of opportunity on the commercial side.

"About thirty years ago the Censorship Act and a new Constitution solidified the government's control of broadcasting. What began as censorship of any printed materials with questionable sexual content, primarily books, was naturally extended to advertising, opinion pieces, theatrical presentations and some reporting, banning anything the board considered improper. As you are now aware, works of some of our favorite authors and playwrights have been banned. We don't dare read your Dr. Spock's baby books. There is virtually no newspaper reporting of sexual crimes. *You* could probably bring a copy of *Playboy* into the country but *I* couldn't buy one here. We wouldn't want any of your liberal western ideas creeping in and challenging our status quo," Tom remarked sarcastically.

"Contraception is the real hot topic. I'm sinning by even saying the word to you. A novel cannot refer to 'The Pill.' We cannot publish an article or advertisement with information about birth control. We have to watch program content carefully for suggestive references, especially in the comedies that are becoming so popular. Our management prefers not to be brought up before the censorship board, so we try to do our own fine-tuned 'editing' before anything is broadcast. That's what would make live reporting from Northern Ireland so tricky; there is no such censorship in place there with the Protestants in control and under British rule." he asked, "Why do you think we're two countries?"

"I didn't realize you were. Isn't Ireland democratic?"

"Yes, in the south we're a democratic republic," Tom tried to explain, "but we have nothing that compares to your idea of free speech. Some say our censorship provisions are similar to those imposed in the Soviet Union. The government might prohibit, but cannot control, the receiving of British national broadcasts, however, so the populace is bombarded with mixed message. That network can film away when a crowd gathers, but we have to be mindful of what the placards say, what the crowds shout and what gestures are used so we can do a quick edit before actual broadcast."

Paula was sitting up cross-legged now too and facing Tom, watching him intently. "I cannot imagine how frustrating that must be both from your standpoint, to have to be so meticulous, and from that of your viewing public, wondering about the bits that have been left out. I have edited myself out of news footage by lowering my head or covering my face whenever the TV cameras came around at a demonstration. But I cannot imagine being on the other end of the camera in such huge emotional crowds and trying to filter anything. And as a viewer I'm sure I wouldn't want that done for me. God Bless America!"

She reasoned, "You have every right to brood as much as you do. It's a wonder I've been able to coax a smile out of you at all."

Tom obliged her with a slight one. "Then take pity on me now and tell me a story. Tell me about San Francisco." He lay back again.

"Truth or tale?"

"Truth, of course, and don't leave anything out."

Still sitting, Paula straightened her blouse at the shoulders and smoothed her skirt. She took a deep breath and began dramatically.

"Once upon a time, in the land of gold nuggets far, far away across the ocean...."

Tom reached a hand behind her and gave her long braid a tug. "I said the truth! I want to hear it all. I want you to speak all those forbidden words. No editing, no censorship allowed!"

"Humor me, then, as I set the stage." She prattled on with slightly less drama in her voice. "World War II is finally over. Europe is rebuilding. America is celebrating by begetting lots and lots of babies. These children, born in the wake of the atomic bomb, come to be known as the 'Baby Boomers' and come of age in the 60's. Many are middle class and begin to question the values and traditions of their parents; they don't want to be like their parents. They flee the strictures of the traditional family. They want to be free to invent themselves and seek tolerance and inclusiveness. They don't care about wealth or societal standing. They want to live in harmony with all of their brothers and sisters, no matter race or creed. And television helps them; television shows them where it's all 'happening.' An alternative youth culture emerges, a 'counterculture.' A 'hippie trail' develops providing food and shelter in college communities as young people move across the country.

"Europe is not an innocent player," Paula glared.

"We shipped you the Beatles and the Rolling Stones, not to mention the mini-skirt," Tom quipped as he gave her hem a little tug.

"We countered with Bob Dylan, the Grateful Dead and tie-dye. Political activism developed on college and university campuses across the country. Most notable among them, Columbia in the east and Berkeley in the west played major roles in the student movement. Similar activities took place all across the states, but the east and west centers drew the largest crowds and got the most national and international publicity.

"Many public campuses were open and anyone, or groups of anyones, could come onto campus and blend right in. All of those bodies seen at student demonstrations weren't necessarily students. They were wannabes, dropouts and runaways as well. There were about 20,000 undergrads at Berkeley when I was there, and a noon gathering might draw 200. The rest of us were in class. We knew that if we dropped out we might not get back in. We couldn't afford *not* to keep going to school. We had goals as much as we had disillusions.

"I was a sophomore at Berkeley at the height of the Free Speech Movement in 1964. As one result of sit-ins, open microphones that could be used by anyone were set up in central areas of campuses. I heard student activists against the war in Vietnam and others for civil rights, poets, longshoreman and philosopher Eric Hoffer, folk singer

Joan Baez, tirades against the relevance of a classical education—a wide range of speakers and performers—while I was there. So it's hard to say it was strictly a student movement.

"Bored silly? You can tell me to stop anytime," she proposed.

"No, not at all. I'm fascinated. I'm just waiting to hear some sinful language."

"Well, here it comes!" Words were spilling out of her now and her hands tried to illustrate as her braid whipped around from side to side. "Activism at Berkeley was largely political, whereas in San Francisco it was not. It was more the peace, love and harmony variety with sex and drugs thrown in. Artistic enclaves existed in many cities—New York, Detroit, Memphis, LA—and especially London—to name a few. Musical experimentation was the name of the game, and Haight-Ashbury near Golden Gate Park is the district where most of these bands congregated in San Francisco. They attracted happy hippie followers who ran bead shops and candle shops and handmade jewelry shops and second hand clothing and furniture shops and drug paraphernalia shops. Remember, they didn't need money; it didn't matter how good they looked or what they wore. Life was 'groovy.' The LA groups were more affluent and private, and in London 'the clothes' and hair were important and the groups tight-knit.

"Marijuana was a dietary staple and LSD was really easy to get until it became illegal in '66 in SF. Everyone shared what he had and when that ran out someone else came along who was willing to share his. The prevalence of drugs made free love easier to come by, and as the consequences began showing up, one house might shelter several men, several women, and an assortment of children of varying ages who were related to some combinations of them all living in communal squalor. Religious or civil marriages were not prerequisite to parenthood. Sometimes a friend who proclaimed himself as having the authority to sanctify a union did the honors and other times it just... well... happened." Her hands came to rest on her hips.

"Are your ears burning yet?" she inquired.

"I'm enthralled. Keep going." Tom was enjoying her commentary and tried to picture Paula among the groups she described.

"Most of the musical groups were self-supporting, but the young people who started to congregate in the Haight didn't have anything to contribute to the community. Not many held regular jobs and not many went to school. They spent their days as I said, tending their shops or making wares for their shops or sitting in doorways along the sidewalks or in groups in the park 'smoking.' One couldn't walk anywhere without stepping over or around some body. Tourist buses began to drive through the area, so some goods were sold and the money used for food and drugs. More and more young people flocked to San Francisco to 'turn on, tune in, and drop out' as the saying goes. These groupies had no thought about how they were going to live; they just wanted to be where it was 'happening.' In the end, when he comes down off his high, a person has got to provide for himself. That's as true for a woman as it is for a man." Paula shot Tom a glance to see how he reacted to that statement. "The music groups— the bands—could make a living, but the majority of the Hippies, kids mostly, couldn't do that. They came with no past, left with no future, and lived for the present and the next 'hit.'

"When feeding the masses became a problem, a group called the Diggers stepped in and tried to provide for everyone in a communal living sort of way. They sought (or took) donations of food from farmer's markets in the city and passed them out for free to all these kids who streamed in and slept any old where. They also had a store that ran on donations where everything was free, even a new identity. There was a section where soldiers could trade a uniform for second hand street clothes. Meanwhile the bands blended rock with folk music and everyone was happy, wore flowers and danced—dances that didn't require steps or partners. Dancing is one of the most profound ways of connecting with another human being, you know," Paula taunted, dancing evocatively from the waist up. Tom laughed at her rendition and wished he felt free enough to join in.

"Last year there were three major events that you might have seen in the news, even here in Ireland." She employed a more instructive tone. "The Hippies staged a 'Be-In' in Golden Gate Park called the 'Gathering of the Tribes' whose purpose was to bring together the 'love' contingent and the activists to share music and the purest acid ever. Timothy Leary, a major player in the psychedelic scene on both coasts, was there, along with about twenty thousand people. In London there was a 'Love-In' in Hyde Park, and in Washington, D.C. there was a huge antiwar demonstration and march on the Pentagon. You might be able to find some old magazine articles with pictures… that is, if they haven't all been censored!" she stated sarcastically. Tom grinned.

"Then, of course, there's last year's 'Summer of Love' in San Francisco which never really materialized as advertised. Police expected the influx of tens of thousands of Hippies for the event. Food and sanitation became a real concern. And, of course, drugs. A free clinic was opened and a twenty-four hour hot line was set up. After the nonevent passed, many of the kids dispersed to the hills and rural areas to the north and along the coast. Others found protest movements throughout the country to join."

"What did your parents think of all this?" Tom asked concerned.

"Probably the worst. But coming away from the 'Summer of Love' with a diploma from a first rate university and enough money in the bank for two years abroad pretty well convinced them I didn't spend all my nights dancing," Paula joked.

"Lord Bedford is turning over Woburn Abbey, his estate outside London, for a 'Festival of the Flower Children' in a couple of weeks. It should be similar to last summer's Monterey International Pop Festival that was so successful. Jimi Hendrix will play, along with Tyrannosaurus Rex, Donovan, and Fleetwood Mac during two days of non-stop music and... whatever. Should be a great time. I plan to be there... purely for purposes of comparison," she teased.

Tom registered disbelief. "A likely story." He folded his arms across his chest and poised himself to interrogate his subject again. "Besides this upcoming 'Festival of the Flower Children,' what have you personally taken part in? Have you ever been arrested?"

She seemed surprised that he would think she had. "I don't have a police record, if that's what you're getting at. In SF, the police tried to enforce an eighteen-year-old age limit at the dance halls, and psychedelics were not illegal until the last couple of years, so neither of those issues applied to me. At Berkeley, I did not take part in the free speech sit-ins, but once the open mike was established I stopped to listen whenever I passed by. I went to a handful of the antiwar rallies on campus. That's where I avoided the news cameras; if I planned to apply for a government job one day I wanted to make sure I could pass the FBI check."

"Where did you live—with the Hippies?" Tom seemed to be taking mental notes.

"In '65 I moved from Berkeley to San Francisco to work while I went to school. I lived not far from the Haight-Ashbury district but certainly not *in* it. I might wander through on a weekend just to see what was happening, but I didn't spend much time there—too many people, too many drugs."

"What kinds of activities *did* you attend?"

"I did go to several dance concerts at the Fillmore Auditorium where dancing to new bands and singers, with strobe lights playing on the walls, was quite the thing. I never felt any fear walking to and from any of these events. One night I went to the Fillmore straight from work so I was in a stylish dress and high heels. There were plenty of other young professionals there just like me, along with the hippie crowd and the antiwar crowd from across the bay. These concerts weren't specific to one group or another. They were cultural opportunities showcasing new as well as known talent around a common theme: what had come before was not acceptable anymore; it was time for social and political change. Janis Joplin sang that night, and the Russian poet Yevgeny Yevtushenko recited some of his political poetry. The ban on his travels outside the Soviet Union had recently been lifted as artists of the sixties sought to crack the Iron Curtain."

"What kinds of demonstrations did you take part in?"

"I marched in a really big antiwar demonstration. Coretta Scott King, Martin Luther King's wife, led the march from the Ferry Building down by the docks all the way up the hill to Golden Gate Park. I was one of about 10,000 who carried placards and sang and then listened to speakers and music all afternoon.

"Is that about the end of your questions, Mr. Reporter?" Paula begged.

"Not likely. How about drugs? Remember this is truth, not tale."

"This won't be particularly interesting," she warned. "I will admit that Berkeley was the incubator for high quality acid production, but that involved a handful of people at most. I was never a part of the drug scene. I was working and going to school. I didn't have the time or the money. I loved the music, loved to play and sing it, loved to dance. I was 'happy' enough doing all that; I didn't need to 'drop acid' to see a kaleidoscope of colors, and too many horror stories of bad 'trips' circulated the scene. Whenever I wondered what I was missing, all I had to do was walk over to the Haight and take a couple of deep breaths to know it wasn't for me. I saw kids transfixed, sitting in doorways or lying on the ground, not even aware of what went on around them."

"Do you mean to tell me—truthfully—that you've never taken drugs?" Tom was incredulous.

"If I were in a group with everyone smoking, when the joint came to me I just passed it along with a smile. No one noticed or cared because they were all stoned. I was never really afraid in those crowds; it was all about peace and harmony. But I did have to be careful what I did. Once, and only once, I accepted some food, a brownie I think, from someone passing a plate around. I knew the minute I ate it that I shouldn't have. Luckily it was only laced with pot; had it been LSD I'd have been out for half a day. THE END," Paula announced with finality.

* * * * *

"Can't be The End," Tom insisted. "You've not told me about Free Love."

She stood up. "I don't intend to. It's not a topic for 'polite conversation,' and even as casual as we've been with one another up to now, I would feel very uncomfortable. Admit it. You would be uncomfortable too. You probably wouldn't dare discuss sex in mixed company."

Tom sensed her unease and sat up to reassure her that he was sincerely interested. "You're not embarrassed? I don't mean to embarrass you. You can be very general. I do not expect specifics about *you*... although I wouldn't mind. You'd do me a service by not turning me loose to make these discoveries on my own."

Paula was surprised by his newfound boldness. She cautioned, "We've already gone way beyond the bounds of what's accepted in your censored society."

"Don't worry about that. There are no cameras or tape recorders hidden in the bushes back there." He pulled her back down to sit beside him and pointed toward the horizon. "There. You can tell your secrets to the sea... and you can pretend I'm not even here."

" 'Free Love' is a misnomer; love is not... free," Paula began thoughtfully. "About the only things free in this life are sunrises and sunsets. Lots of the young people who gathered in San Francisco wanted to flaunt their newfound sexual freedom, regardless of consequence. Some maintained exclusive partners; others didn't. They went from partner to partner or just picked up someone whenever they were in the mood. Contraceptives were available but not always used; thus disease and pregnancy were widespread. Sex could take place anytime of the day or night, whenever the spirit moved." Paula's graphic descriptions disgusted and delighted Tom at the same time.

Her eyes fixed on the ocean, she continued. "Sex wasn't restricted to a bedroom. In a communal living situation, a bedroom might be set aside in a house for... that, sometimes for whoever was 'head' and his 'woman.' And the rest of the group found other convenient places. No one paid much attention. Interestingly, on campuses now, students are pushing for co-ed dorms. These 'flower children' were definitely not shy about expressing affection... if there were any true affection. An equal amount of drug inducement was probably mixed in. Along the streets, in doorways and in the park you could see couples with hands all over the place groping each other, lips locked, and sometimes more. They appeared to me to do it because they could; they never thought of it as sinful.... I don't suppose that would go over very well here?" Paula turned toward Tom to gauge his reaction.

He reacted vehemently. "Absolutely not! Public displays of affection are *not* condoned. Even after marriage public displays are kept to a minimum—only what's considered polite. For us young people only a pat or handshake, maybe an arm-in-arm outside, is allowed. People will talk otherwise and word will get back to the parents and maybe as far as the parish priest."

"That sounds absolutely boring! But it tells me that you are in a great deal of trouble, lying out here in public view in the sun with a girl, a stranger at that, whose hair you pull and whose hand and face you touch and whose forbidden words you soak in. Admit it," Paula challenged. "We'd never be having this conversation in a pub in Dublin. We probably wouldn't even be *seen* together in a pub in Dublin."

Tom would not admit out loud that she was right. He would not be seen in public like this—alone with a female companion—unless they were related or had a 'formal understanding.' "I'd be proud to be seen with you anywhere, even in a pub. And don't you worry about my soul. I'm keeping count of the sins I commit. I'll not let it go too far," he said with a reassuring smile.

"I worried most about the children." Paula grew pensive. "Communal living sounds great in theory. Everyone looking out for everyone else. Everyone sharing. Mutual love and respect. They all sound great, but in practice I saw something very different. I saw a lot of scruffy, dirty young people, lots of idealism, and no specific goals. Cleaning didn't seem to get done, even with all those helping hands living together. Sometimes a house only had one bathroom, and twelve or more adults lived there. Children may have had one mother and one father, but they were frequently shared and raised communally. They were born into a drug-thick atmosphere and plenty of filth to go along with it. Midwifery came back into style."

Tom interjected, "We have communal living here too. It's called a family. In the bigger cities like Dublin there are lots of families who live in close quarters. A father, a mother and maybe eight to twelve children live in a couple of bedrooms, a living room and kitchen, and the bathroom may even be outside or shared with other families. Dirty comes with the territory."

"I can't imagine choosing that lifestyle."

"Oh, they don't choose it; they're born into poverty and can't move themselves up."

"Why do they have such large families, then?"

"That's a matter for themselves and the church fathers to work out."

Paula began to editorialize. "Well, living communally, in a big house or sitting around a campfire or in a park singing, smoking and feeling all those good vibes may be great for some, health issues aside, but I'm kind of partial to strong soap and hot water and having my own space. I can't imagine raising children with several other parents. It seems to me that a child ought to know who his parents are. Who defines his code of behavior. Who is responsible for him. Where his own space is. Where he will sleep at night. A child ought to be able to depend on certain things. There are some 'families' that just roll up in a blanket together to sleep under the stars and call that home.

"I hope this rant won't give you nightmares," she added.

"Not likely. So *did* you?   Sit around campfires and sing and smoke?" asked Tom.

"If you've been listening, you already know I wasn't into smoking—not even banana peels," Paula stated firmly.

"Oh, I'm listening. I just thought to catch you in a tale!" Tom joshed.

"I have been known to strum along and sing a chorus or two," she replied modestly.

"Really?"

"In San Francisco, everyone played guitar—badly perhaps, but everyone sang and played." Paula jiggled with animation now.   "I bought my first guitar with earnings from a summer job after my freshman year in college. Your English cousins the Rolling Stones and the Beatles had just 'invaded' and their rock melodies were simple to pick up and easy to dance to. Folk music was all the rage on campuses and in coffeehouses. The beauty of a folk song was that anyone could easily sing it. To play, all one needed was the ability to keep time and to finger a few basic chords." She remembered, "You play piano, right?"

"Everyone plays piano."

"Then you know how far a few simple chords will take you. In San Francisco, everyone played and/or sang. Music was portable. A guitar, banjo, ukulele or harmonica could be carried along easily."

Boring right into his eyes, she continued. "Songs can at least move the world if not change it, which is what's happening now. Folk singers perform in coffeehouses on the west and east coast—San Francisco, Harvard Square, Greenwich Village, LA, Monterey. We're hearing lots of message songs which tell us to come together, love one another, we are not alone, etc. 'We Shall Overcome' is a good example. These songs were not meant to be entertainment. They were conceived to spread a message, to be anthems for change.

"Music transcends economic levels and breaks down cultural barriers; therefore, it is able to cross traditional, ethnic, racial and religious lines. Many musicians and singers are political activists as much as they are performers. Music of protest and politics, human injustice, hope and love is so important to the Civil Rights movement in America and the anti-war movement and to the 'Hippies' who proclaim peace and love... all because of music's ability to appeal beyond one group or one style."

Paula took the ogham stone paper and a pencil from her skirt pocket and turned Tom around so she could use his back to write on while she resumed. "The next time you're in London on business you need to take an extra day, or even half a day, and spend it in a record shop just listening to American music. I'll make you a list of bands and artists, and maybe some banned magazines you should look at too, to complete your picture of America in the sixties."

Her touch on his shoulder and her hand moving across his back felt foreign and familiar to him at the same time. "Ah, London," he reflected. "My source for all things condemned and obscene."

"Not every young person sees the sixties through the same lens. The European experience is different from the American experience, and San Francisco is just one example." Paula grew pensive again. "I started this decade with a handshake from Pres. John F. Kennedy and in just the few years since, I've seen his assassination, MLK's and Bobby Kennedy's assassinations, kids come home broken or dead from an insupportable war, San Francisco turned over to flower children with no personal goals, blacks fighting for civil rights, women fighting for equal rights, and music gone wild. Now we're ready to send a man to the moon. What a study in contrasts!

"I really don't think the divergent movements can sustain themselves too much longer—maybe another year or so—in a peaceful, non-violent way. Peace and love will give way to antiwar and civil rights where the real emotions and just cause lie. Vietnam was a young person's protest that has lately become everyone's war. Our ideals will give way to realities, and I'm afraid non-violence will give way to violence because emotions are strung so tightly," she expounded further.

"I saw that in Paris in May following the police's eviction of students from a sit-in. They were just protesting the authoritarian education system." Paula recalled the recent disturbing incident and became dramatic again, ceasing her writing while she continued the story. "Sitting in a café across from the Sorbonne enjoying a spring day, I saw a few students, then more and more, running up the boulevard. I turned toward the river and saw police in full riot gear shoulder to shoulder across the breadth of the street. They wore helmets and what looked like bulletproof jackets and carried shields and clubs and advanced steadily toward the students. The students used bricks and stones, and we bystanders were caught in the middle with nowhere to go. My friend and I dashed down the street, around a corner, down another street and into an alley. Then we tried to walk calmly to the nearest metro station and leave. I never saw anything like *that* in the Bay Area, but some of the civil rights demonstrations at home are becoming violent now, too."

"Aren't civil rights for Negroes late in coming to the United States? I thought your Civil War was fought a hundred years ago," Tom asked as he tried to turn to face her.

Paula squared his shoulders and finished her thoughts and her list. "Rights don't necessarily follow from wars. Are our internal problems so different from your troubles with the Protestants in the North, or class divisions so evident in Dublin? You should get your own house in order before you question the way we're trying to repair ours. And, for future reference, that term is falling out of favor now."

She handed the list over his shoulder. He glanced at it, nodding and chuckling at some of her notes (Music: listen to the WORDS. *Rolling Stone*: the magazine, not the band. *Playboy*: Skip the photos. Read the articles. *Ramparts*: May be hard to find. You'll never believe it started as a Catholic literary mag!). Then he put the list in his pocket, got up, reached for her hands, and pulled her to standing too, a bit closer than seemed appropriate. They stood studying each other like this for some time.

Tom wrestled between what he wanted to say and what was proper. Finally, he let out a sigh and asked, "Hungry? Let's grab some pub grub and a pint and expose you to more of the local color."

Reluctant to accept, she said, "This would be the second meal in a row you've offered. Should I be worried?" She could see Tom's answer in his eyes rolled upward. "You've already been more than generous. You're certainly not obliged to take care of me as if I were some homeless waif or one of your little sisters."

"Nonsense. I have in mind a cultural experience for you tonight. Let's see how we Irish compare to the Yugoslavs or your American coffeehouses for fun and frolic."

Since she had not enough skirt to keep pulled down to an acceptable level, Paula suggested, "A gentleman wouldn't be seen in public with the likes of me in this state. I'd better run change into something more modest so I don't embarrass you further or get myself arrested for indecency in this conservative Irish village of yours. We wouldn't want *that* to get back to your Aunt Moira."

"Don't bother. The fellows like seeing a bit of leg and will soon be too drunk to remember that they have." Tom guided her along to the road, running his hand up and down her back with smug surprise on his face. As they passed by a cottage on the way to the pub, he plucked a wild yellow rose from its bush and wove it carefully into her long braid. "There. Now you look like a real American Hippie."

Chapter 5

O'Hanlon's and Dunbar's were the two pubs in the village. Tom and Paula entered O'Hanlon's and were greeted by the man himself, or Jr., standing behind the bar handing out the pints. *"Céad míle fáilte*, Mr. Thomas!" he shouted. "Heard ye were here. Glad yer joinin' us."

"Best music in town, Sean. You still serving up supper?"

"Sure."

"Grand.... Sean, I'd like you to meet my friend from America, Miss Paula. Paula, Sean here and his father have run this establishment for maybe thirty-five years?"

"Thirty-seven, Mr. Thomas. Me father doesn't come in so much anymore though. Mostly early in a day. Nice to finally meet ye, Miss Paula. We heard ye was in town with Mr. Thomas here." He raised his right hand, snapped his fingers and pointed to a table in the corner by a window and the fireplace. The men who were there immediately got up and took their pints with them to the long wooden table down the center of the large room. A third-generation boy, too small for the apron wrapped around him, wiped the table clean and set the chairs straight.

The crowd parted and nodded to them as Tom ushered his guest to their place, the best in the house again. His favored dry stout followed and was on the table before they were seated. The planked floor and oak bar were highly polished, and dark wooden beams spanned the ceiling's breadth. The walls were wood-paneled below and whitewashed above. Amber windowpanes mellowed the sharp contrast. Four stools stood empty on the other side of the fireplace. Instruments rested against them. An olive-colored eight-foot Atlantic halibut was arched over the mantle of the fireplace with his two right-sided eyes staring down at their table. Logs were laid but not burning, probably waiting for a rainy evening. The bar took up one whole side of the room, several stools along its front. Behind, pints were stacked on one side of the draught and glasses on the other. Famed Irish whiskey bottles were lined up beside those. Half a dozen tables bordered the outside wall, and chairs were scattered everywhere; although tonight, patrons seemed to outnumber them. Paula noticed that those patrons seemed to be only men and they seemed to be ogling her. She should have insisted on changing into pants.

As they sipped their hearty brew, another group of five entered, two guys and three girls probably from the hostel. They shoved two tables together and rearranged the seating to suit themselves, haggling over who would sit where. They looked as out of place as Paula felt.

"You stinker!" she charged Tom. "You're just trying to challenge my thesis."

"What thesis is that?"

"That we'd never be seen together in a Dublin pub. This may not be Dublin, but it surely is male dominated enough to be, even though I don't see any sign that says 'no women allowed.' All these men seem to know you... and me, for that matter. Where are my long pants when I need them!"

He chuckled at her apprehensions. "You worry too much about appearances. That's my job. I'll take care of this." He rose with his pint in his hand. The entire pub grew quiet, and Tom began to speak.

"Nice to see you again. Johnny O'... Daniel... Robbie..." He nodded an acknowledgement to several others as well, and they all nodded back. "As you know, my father was a Kerry man. You may not know that my mother is a Fitzgerald from over to Cork. Well, it is indeed a pleasure for my American friend Miss Paula and myself to join you for some song and dance tonight. She's anxious for a grand *ceilidh*, so we know you'll put your hearts to it. Paula was once honored by a good Irish handshake from none other than our dear departed brother, President John Fitzgerald Kennedy."

The crowd all cried, "Hear! Hear!" and raised their glasses.

"I'm sure you will accord her your hospitality and the same to our other traveling friends," gesturing to the group next to them. "Drinks all around, Sean." He raised his glass to them, shouted "*sláinte!*" and sat down. The noise was deafening for a moment as glasses were pounded on the tables and bar and thanks were shouted. Paula heard mutterings and comments of disbelief, and the gawking turned from her legs to her now famous right hand.

"That was quite an announcement," she said. "I'm not sure whether I'm more embarrassed now than I was before."

"You'll be real popular tonight," he laughed. "They'll all be wanting to dance with you just to touch your favored hand!"

She was surprised that idolatrous feelings for the Kennedys pervaded the country. "Is your mother really related to the Kennedys?"

"I haven't a clue. I never said she was."

Paula had to smile at his ruse. "Serves me right for doubting that your intentions were honorable."

Tom had not ordered, but their food appeared nonetheless. Bangers and Mash. The huge sausages tasted as if they were boiled in ale and the mashed potatoes contained bits of onion and cabbage. Yummy! she thought. I do not have to guess what this is.

Just as they started to eat, one of the hostlers approached their table. "Excuse me, but could you help us?" he asked in a thick southern accent. "We can't tell from the menus. Is there anything like a hamburger on here?"

Tom tried to contain his smile and answered, "The closest would be this: minced meat and a bap, and chips. That's French fries."

"Thanks. And what's that?" pointing to their plates.

"This is 'bangers and mash.' The sausages are cooked in ale and very good."

"Looks good. Um…What are you drinking?"

"This is our world-famous stout. It's a traditional drink around here. It's very thick and very hearty—only a bit stronger than your beer." He raised his pint for inspection. "Been traveling long?"

"We just flew in to Shannon this morning and rented a car. We heard this was a neat place to stay, so we came here first. We've been on the road most of the day, so we're really hungry."

"Well, you'll want to stick around for a while tonight. Pretty soon there will be music and dancing. Should be an entertaining evening."

"Thanks. We'll think about it." And he returned to his table to discuss orders with his companions.

"My pleasure. Enjoy your visit." Tom turned to his guest with admiration on his face. "Paula, you are such a treasure! You are so easy to please. Who comes all the way to Ireland for a hamburger?"

"Need you ask?"

In between bites he inquired, "So, what will you be doing five years from now? Will you be at a Dublin pub with me eating bangers and mash and dancing an Irish jig?"

"I have no idea. After one more year traveling and then graduate school for at least another two, I should be just getting started in the world of work. Or I may be in the Peace Corps—depends on Chuck. If he can stay out of the war somehow, then I'll volunteer for a two-year stint making 'peace.' One of us should give national service, but we don't both want to be locked into an overseas commitment at the same time. If it's a choice between war and peace, I'll opt for peace every time."

She caught his glance and arched her eyebrow. "So, depending on where I am in this world five years from now, maybe I can fit a visit to a Dublin pub with you into my summer plans… if you impress me with your dancing tonight, that is."

He chuckled. "Why would a woman need a graduate degree?"

"To get a job good enough to support a family. To be prepared for whatever comes. To contribute in a meaningful way to her community. You said a job is validation for a man, validation of his ability to provide properly for his family. Why would it be less so for a woman?"

"A married woman wouldn't need to provide for the family. The husband takes the care."

"That assumes marriage. But marriage and economics aside, what of personal fulfillment?"

"That comes from family—husband and children."

"Are there no women in your employ?"

"Yes, a few, but they are older, single, widowed for the most part."

"So a woman's work outside the home is a last-ditch effort, so to speak, to keep her off the streets?"

"Work is a measure of a *man's* worth, *his* ability to provide. You make it seem so harsh."

"Your attitude *is* harsh. A woman has as much right as a man to self-fulfillment be it from work or family. You wouldn't want your wife to feel stilted in your marriage would you?"

"But work might take her from her responsibilities to her home and her family. She mightn't have enough time left to devote to them."

"Then, maybe the husband would have to help out!" Paula gave him a saucy smile.

"You won't find *me* changing nappies and straightening the playroom!" was Tom's retort. They both laughed heartily as they finished their frothy ale and more was set before them.

"Seriously, Paula." He clinked her glass and leaned forward across the table to invite her attention. "You are an enigma."

At her surprise, he explained further, "I mean, I don't know any girls who express themselves so freely—who would *dare* to challenge a man's opinion—like you have. It's just not done here."

"So, I *do* fit your stereotype…"

"Not at all! I find you very… refreshing… and I shouldn't even say that much."

* * * * *

They took turns excusing themselves to freshen up before the entertainment began. Tom stopped by the bar and talked to O'Hanlon, gesturing toward the musicians' station. He took a roll of bills and counted them out to the host probably covering dinner, the rest of the evening and maybe the whole party. Then he disappeared around the corner of the bar.

As the musicians were getting settled, two young Irishmen who politely introduced themselves as Johnny O' and Daniel approached Paula. They were representative of the group assembled. Their attire was well worn but clean, probably their Sunday best minus jackets and caps. Shirtsleeves were slightly rolled above wrists, and heavy belts or suspenders secured pants. Faces and hands were scrubbed clean, the faces glowing red from drink. Hair was slicked back with the popular oil of the day, a comb's course still evident. Most wore heavy shoes or clean black work boots. The largely male crowd was also older. The younger were the industrious ones who had fishing boats of their own. Many of their peers had moved to Dublin or immigrated across the sea in search of a decent living, Paula later learned.

Apparently Johnny O' and Daniel were the bravest of the present lot and were commissioned by the others to learn the tale of the "handshake." Paula obliged by telling them that she attended a rally when Kennedy campaigned for president and had the privilege of meeting him after his speech. She tried not to embellish too much the intensity in his eyes, the genuineness of his smile, or the warmth and heartiness of his grasp. Yes, she could still feel the touch of his hand as if it were yesterday.

The musicians tuned up in the background behind the noise of the crowd. Tom returned with his sweater over his shoulders, his starched shirt unbuttoned two more notches and his sleeves rolled to his elbows. Now with a fresh drink in hand, he looked as if he were loosening up. He scooted his chair to sit at Paula's side of the table in their front row seats near the band. He rested his arm on the back of her chair. "The better to view the group," he explained. Paula thought he might have some "fun" in him after all and looked forward to the rest of the evening.

Four musicians were surrounded by nearly twice as many instruments. One would be playing the Uilleann pipes and the penny whistle. Another was the percussionist with traditional bones, spoons and a bodhran positioned conveniently around him. A third would alternate between guitar and banjo, and the last was the fiddler. The music began with a song everyone seemed to know, for they all sang "Black Velvet Band." It was followed by "Whiskey in the Jar" and "Galway Bay." The combo then played a tune Paula had heard before in one of the singing pubs of Dublin, so she knew what to do and grabbed her glass. One young man played the rover by singing the solo verses, and all joined in the chorus, banging their glasses in rhythm on the tables and bar when it came time—"bang... tap, tap... bang!"

The music and singing continued until the fiddler quieted the crowd and announced that in honor of their guests tonight, the band would play a couple of old familiar tunes so the visitors would feel comfortable in singing along. After that there would be a short break while the room was cleared for dancing.

"John Jacob Jingleheimer Smith" began slowly to a whisper, each repeat of the chorus becoming faster and louder until finally the fiddler outdid himself and no one could keep up with him. The group erupted in gales of laughter, then became suddenly maudlin as they joined in "When Irish Eyes Are Smilin'," the tenor voices competing to see who could hold that high-note "hearts" the longest. Rousing applause followed as the band took its leave.

Glasses were set in the windowsills, on the mantle and on the bar as tables and chairs were pushed to the side. The long center table was moved to the back across the far end of the room clearing space for dancing. Once the music resumed with traditional Irish jigs, it seemed strange to see no female partners. That did not stop the young men, as dance they did. The alcohol flowed as freely as the music, though Paula gave up trying to match the others.

At the beginning of the third dance, Tom led her to the floor and after a round or two she was able to pick up the footwork well enough. Then he passed her off to Daniel who was honored to take her right hand. Tom brought one of the hostlers out and cajoled the others to join in the fun. He danced once with each of the American girls and then handed them off to others. Paula decided it was not the dancing; it was the pumping up and down of her right arm that was wearing her out as she went from partner to new partner as well. They danced jigs to "The Fluter's Ball" and "Dear Old Donegal" and waltzed to an up tempo version of "When Irish Eyes Are Smilin'."

At last, the couple found themselves together again, but just for a moment, previous formality long gone. "Come away with me to Dublin, Paula," he smiled and twirled her into the arms of another. At their next pass a few seconds later, he had her in a firm grasp, sang to her as if she were a "rover" and decreed, "No more!" before he was cut in on again. On their third partnering, he recited a little too exuberantly for her comfort, "Is it conscience holds me back, or courage that I lack? / Both, or either, keep me from… telling you, 'I'm glad you've come… into my life.' "

Hmm. Tom waxes poetic when he's had too much of the Irish water, she thought.

Before he could continue, a face that was not his leaned close to Paula's ear and cautioned, "A girl can get pregnant from dancin' ye know." She thanked it for the warning as its body snatched her away from her lyrical escort.

When the jigs subsided and a sentimental ballad began, Tom found her again, surrounded her with his arms, rested his head on her shoulder and nuzzled her neck gently. In more of a sway than a true step, they continued like this long enough for her to feel his contentment as he held her. She wondered who would be leading whom back to the hostel this night and hoped she remembered the way.

He framed Paula's face in his hands, gazed intently into her eyes and said, "I meant it, you know," and enveloped her again into his embrace, drawing her ever closer while trying to keep time to the strains of "The Rose of Tralee." The entire company swaying and singing to "I'll Take You Home Again, Kathleen" signaled the end of the session. Then they maundered out of the pub in two's and three's, humming as they left.

Tom made his way to the musicians' corner to thank them personally for adapting their program for his guest and the other Americans. Their pleasure at his attention was obvious, punctuated as it was by handshakes and slaps on the back.

Among the last to leave, the couple walked arm-in-arm back to the hostel. This time, before she could get the words out, he thanked *her* for an enlightening day and a wonderful evening and hoped they might "dance the night away" again. She shook her head gently, "Unless you're planning on a trip to Galway tomorrow, I'm afraid this is goodbye."

"You're not leaving… so soon?"

"I'd planned on it. My bedroll and clothes should finally be dry."

"Give them another day, just to be sure," he appealed. Then ever so gently, he tilted her face to his and kissed her on the forehead.

* * * * *

Paula showered, packed her laundry away and fell into bed to reflect on her day, but sleep descended before she could.

Chapter 6

The next morning Paula went to the desk to make arrangements with Alfie for checking out. He handed her another post card, this time one of funny looking birds on a rock. On it was simply scrawled,

Dock
10:00
Swimsuit
T.

Surprise! Rather presumptive of him, she thought, to expect her to forego *her* plans for *his* impish pleasure, but again Paula was intrigued and headed back to the dorm. If she left by mid-afternoon, she could still get a jump on the long trip to Galway.

Swimsuit. Cutoffs. T-shirt. Hair? Ponytail. Jacket? Maybe. Towel? No. Paula was not going to sacrifice her freshly laundered towel to the sand, mud, grass, salt water, whatever. Tom better come prepared for both of them. Shoes? Preferable to sandals. No telling where they might be headed, and she did not want to be slipping and sliding if she needed to make a quick getaway. She asked herself, if I think I might need to make a quick getaway, why am I even going? Answer: Why not?

She grabbed her day-old rolls and a cup of tea from the communal pot in the kitchen. Tea did not taste the same from a paper cup, she admitted. Then she headed for the dock.

She found Tom and a friend readying a boat. They were not to go sailing for it had no mast or sails. A fishing boat maybe, but there did not seem to be gear out, and it was a bit late to get started for that. She was fearful that this might be a diving boat; she had never done that before.

When he spied Paula walking toward them, he waved her over and helped her onto the vessel. "You're right on time. Glad you wore shoes." (She expected a "Hi! I didn't know if you'd come. Glad to see you.") He took one look at the paper cup in her hand, shook his head muttering "Oh, no, Paula," and removed it firmly from her grasp. "That's not the proper way to drink tea!" He retrieved a dirty mug from the bottom of the boat and wiped it out with the hem of his sweatshirt. He poured the hot liquid into the mug and thrust it toward her. "Here." And he tossed the paper cup into the trash. Then he released the aft line, pulled it in and they were off.

Des was a friend from summers during their teen years working on fishing boats. Paula met him the previous night at O'Hanlon's. He nodded a good morning, dressed in what looked like his Sunday best except for his rolled up shirtsleeves and his hat. His suit coat was slung over the wheel. "We're in a bit of a hurry here. Des is due back for 11 o'clock Mass, so he has just enough time to drop us off and return."

"Drop us off where" was on Paula's mind as all she could see, save for the island quickly disappearing behind them, was sea and more sea. Tom was in his grey sweats. As she eyed him up and down, she asked "And you're not going with him?"

"I've already been. I haven't attended Mass so early in the morning since I was a schoolboy! Now, come over here and let's get your jacket on. It's going to be a cool windy ride." She let him help her; then she listened quietly as the two men recounted misadventures from a few years past. They seemed to be enjoying themselves as the boat sped southward.

Their destination became evident when Des turned the boat east toward dramatic craggy cliffs which jutted some 500 feet out of the water. From sea level they loomed above the adventurers with no apparent debarking possible. Their pilot maneuvered the boat around to the northeast and cut the motor.

"Des thinks the sea is calm enough today that he can get us on," said Tom as he slung a rolled blanket looped through a basket over his shoulders and across his chest. As the boat inched closer, he stepped on its rail and sprang to the cliff, hugging his body to it until he could steady his footing on a ledge. Then he clambered up twenty vertical feet of rock face to a barely perceptible track of gradual ascent saying, "I'll be back for you in a minute."

Paula felt the pitching of the boat as she watched Tom disappear over the top of the rock. She stared at the wall of stone in front of her. It was dotted with outcroppings, protrusions of rock that looked dangerously like knife blades thrusting out toward her. She imagined her body splattered against the stone wall, food for birds and grist for a news story.

She could see the headline now: "UNKNOWN BODY IMPALED ON ISLAND. Local fishermen discovered the body of a young woman impaled on a rock outcropping on the east side of an island off the west coast of Ireland. The body is believed to be that of the species *touriste americansus* because it had stripes common to those who bask in the sun at their leisure; however, no ID was found."

Paula cursed herself for leaving her ID in her locker, but there were not many places to stow it in a swimsuit. And, of course, no one knew where she was; no one would come looking for her.

"Authorities are puzzled as to how the body arrived at the spot about four m. above high tide line. Perhaps a huge wave deposited it there even though no evidence of drowning was found. No evidence of foul play was found either. No missing persons matching the description of the body have been reported in the area. A local Valentia Island resident suggested, quote, 'Americans think they can do anything, even fly.' Investigation will continue as soon as local authorities resolve the dispute involving Mrs. Daughtry's missing cow which was found in Mr. O'Hara's goat shed."

Tom's head reappeared, and then the rest of him, without the basket. He descended until he was on a narrow ledge just above the spot where he landed safely moments before. He crouched down and took the blanket from around his chest, fashioning a loop at each end. He slid his left hand through one and gripped the blanket with it, letting go the other end. He motioned for Paula to grab the empty loop and do the same with her right. She did.

"Whatever you do, don't let go," Tom shouted toward the boat. "Now, when I tell you to jump, jump straight toward the rock and grab my right wrist with your other hand as tightly as you can. I'll hold you 'til you can find your footing. Then you can let go my wrist and we'll climb up. But don't let go the blanket 'til we get to the top, no matter what."

Des steadied her on the railing, and when the boat rode the crest of a small wave inward, they both yelled, "Jump!" and she did. The next thing she felt was not a splat against the rock but the strength of Tom's hand as he grabbed her wrist. Then jerked quickly upward, she felt as if a crane had hoisted her, so steady and strong was his grasp. She found the ledge and her breath and followed him carefully from foot hole to notch to hole up the wall until they reached the obscure path. He led her over the top with the blanket wrapped around them.

If Paula was petrified, he could not tell. "Good job. You're really game for just about anything, aren't you?" he said. "Sit down a minute and catch your breath." He waved to Des to signal their safe arrival, and she heard the boat rev up and speed away.

* * * * *

"Welcome to Puffin Island, named for its primary inhabitant the Arctic Puffin," he announced.

So this must be the sacred Puffin Island of Tom's youth, Paula thought. She looked from one side of the narrow island to the other and could see why. There were birds everywhere, black and white birds about a foot in length with grey cheeks, red-orange legs and large curved bills. Some of them were waddling on their webbed feet, wings outspread to about twenty-four inches, emitting a deep growl toward the intruders.

"They won't bother us as long as we don't disturb their nests," Tom continued. "This is their nesting season. The birds build shelters in the rocks and in burrows left by the rabbits." Paula looked more closely and saw as many rabbits popping in and out of holes as she did birds.

"These clown birds spend most of their lives on the sea, even mating there. Then they come here to build their nests, hatch their chicks and care for them for a few weeks until the chicks fledge and fly or swim back out to sea. The whole process takes about three months. Mum and dad mate for life when they are 4 or 5 years old, and both share in the care of the nest and the feeding. During mating they grow a black, white, blue, orange and red striped plate covering their bills. That's why they're referred to as 'clowns of the ocean.' They tap their bills together while courting, and then when the deed is done they shed the plates. We might be able to find some scattered on the rocks and in the grass, so watch your step. Because their bills are so big, they are able to catch and hold as many as a dozen fish at a time using their tongues to secure them against their palates.

"The rabbits.... Well, you know about rabbits. The island is only about a half mile wide by a mile long, so it can get very crowded here during breeding season. We should be able to find a patch of grass big enough for the two of us, though, and hope we can keep the rabbits from ransacking our picnic lunch." Tom found such a spot up over a knoll and just south of center. "The sunny side," he said. He set down the basket and blanket, then led Paula back up to the top of the knoll.

"I can understand how sea birds fly in and nest here, but where do you suppose the rabbits came from?" she asked.

"They could swim from the mainland, I guess. It's only about a quarter of a mile," he explained. "But it's more likely they came by boat, maybe from shipwreck on the rocks or stowaways on fishing vessels. It doesn't take many rabbits to get a colony started."

Tom stood behind Paula, took her by the shoulders, and righted her to what he called 'true north.' "Every time I come here, I orient myself to the four cardinal points of the compass and imagine all the possibilities that lie beyond this rock. If you look directly north, you'll pass through the North Pole and then on to the Soviet Union." He turned her an exact ninety degrees clockwise and directed her gaze beyond Great Britain to Denmark, Germany and Poland. Again they rotated another ninety. He placed his right arm on her shoulder and his point passed the coast of Portugal and continued to Morocco.

Finally they oriented due west and he indicated the border between Newfoundland and Quebec.

"You live in Colorado, right?" he remembered.

"Yes, about 700 miles south of the Canadian border."

Tom shifted them some fifteen degrees south of west, and his left arm joined his right around her face. He shot a fictive arrow along the great circle route which intersected Newfoundland, skimmed the southern tip of Hudson Bay and the north end of Lake Superior, then passed through South Dakota and Nebraska before coming to rest in the wheat fields of Colorado. "This is the westernmost point of Europe, you know, the closest you'll be to home for another year."

Paula doubted his geography but liked the sound of it and spent some time shouting messages homeward. Tom encircled her snugly around the midriff and rested his chin on her shoulder as she channeled her thoughts and words toward "Mom and Daddy, Chuck and her best friend from high school Teresa who wrote she was having trouble with her boyfriend." He laughed at her silliness but was beguiled by it. She covered his arms with her own, and he clutched her even more tightly.

"Look at the ocean," Paula directed. "Look at the undulant sea green waves as far as the eye can see. Now, close your eyes. Replace the blue-green with amber and you'll see the fields of ripening grain that fill my vistas. You cannot understand 'vast' until you see the prairies of the west—a geometry of green and golden fields, like a patchwork quilt stretching to the horizon.... I do miss it sometimes."

Barely loosening his hold on her, Tom turned their backs on the west and guided her to their spot on the downside of the knoll. He drew her in tightly again and, nudging her ponytail aside with his nose, brought his lips to the back of her neck.

Up to now Tom's advances were cautious, Paula thought. His familiarity while they were dancing the previous night could be attributed to the alcohol. Now his approaches were overstepping the bounds of public display set by his strict religious upbringing. She worried about what that would imply to any witness, then realized that this day the only witnesses to his indiscretions were the birds and the rabbits.

With a sigh, he released his hold and gave her a pat on the rear. "Strip down and give me your clothes," he commanded.

"What!" Paula barked at him defiantly. He was so guarded until now that she did not expect such a bold move. A new headline flashed through her mind: "Body Found Ravaged Atop Island." It was stupid to allow herself to become so isolated, and she worried how she might extricate herself from this predicament.

"Don't go goosey on me now. Get down to your swimsuit so we can hit the water. Leave your shoes on."

Paula could tell by the hurt in Tom's eyes that he understood what she assumed, and she was embarrassed by her jump to a faulty conclusion.

He was out of his sweats in a flash. Under all those starched shirts and bulky sweaters he camouflaged a strong stocky prizefighter's body. His trunk was a triangle of broad shoulders and burly chest that narrowed to a slight waist. His well-defined biceps were twice the size of hers and his legs, short in proportion to the rest of his body, looked to be made of spring steel.

"Do you box?" she asked.

"Most school boys learn to," he replied. "It's a matter of survival. Give me your clothes so I can wrap them up, to keep the sand out if it blows." She helped Tom roll all of their clothes together in the blanket, then he tied it around and over the top of the basket that held their lunch. "To keep the rabbits out."

Waves of salty sea grass arched to shelter grains of sand. If they were gathered all together on a beach, the sand would be black. Here it was charcoal grit, permeating everything, blown in from nearby islands and the product of erosion of the craggy cliffs. Tom thought Paula looked deliciously indecent, clad as she was in almost nothing and her knees smudged with the fine-grained grey powder.

His eyes dropped to the ground. "Your shoes," he said. "You'll need them to walk back and forth. Sharp rocks are hidden beneath the sand and grass." He shed his hurt as he grabbed her hand and headed them to the south end of the island, rabbits and puffins skittering out of the way.

* * * * *

"As far as I've been able to discover, there's but one safe pathway down to the water aside from where the boat put in." They left their shoes at the top and peered over the edge. Below, Paula saw a large pool approximately 250 feet in diameter encircled with rock which formed a sort of barrier and broke all but the fiercest waves. She was not too keen on climbing down a rock wall after that morning's harrowing climb up, but learned that she was not expected to. This time they would jump!

A barely visible trail took them part way down, but it turned into sharp rock and became steeper. She decided that jumping would actually be preferable. Tom explained that they could not come onto the island this way because a boat could not pass the rock barrier, and they would be forced to swim in. He splashed down first and then motioned for her to follow. He reminded her to jump out, not down.

Paula took a deep breath, closed her eyes and jumped, her ponytail trailing behind her. She expected to feel an icy rush up her nose when she hit the ocean, but she did not. The water was relatively warm, and Tom could tell she was pleasantly surprised. "It's the Gulf Stream current brings warm water this way. It seems to pool up here on this side of the island so the sun can give it an extra shot of heat too." He took her hand and pulled her down beneath the surface and over to where sea plants were growing in abundance, clinging to the rocks and waving with the motion of the water. The swimmers came up for air and went down again and again so he could point out all the varieties and tell her about them. They also discovered tiny crabs and mussels clinging to the rocks with shrimp floating nearby.

Tom wanted to swim out to the barrier to show Paula how he managed to get onto Puffin Island when he was alone. She took hold of his ankle and let him do all the work swimming them there against the current. He felt around the easternmost end of the arc and finally located a hook he implanted several years before. He would tie up his boat there and then swim across the pool to gain access to the island carrying his gear along in a plastic. He had to watch the tides carefully when he did. He could become stranded if the boat floated into the pool on a high tide where he could not get it out again or if a rough sea bashed it against the rocks.

He dove deeper and loosened a large rock, reaching in behind it to retrieve a rusted waterproof tin. He unscrewed the top and displayed its contents—some matches and a whistle. "My emergency kit," he laughed. "Just like all good scouts, I thought I needed an emergency kit. I don't know what I intended for fuel for a fire or who would hear the whistle, but they seemed like a good idea at the time." He replaced the top and the tin and the rock. "Just in case we get stranded."

The two swam lazily back to the center of the pool. They were the only otters out that day, cavorting playfully, dunking and wrestling with one another, diving and clambering for sinking rocks. Their bodies coming together in play seemed so natural. Neither her strength nor her stroke could match his, but they behaved as a pair nonetheless. They could not move so freely without the protection of the barrier; the currents would be too strong.

The exhilaration that comes with physical exertion relaxed their inhibitions. They played a game of Hide and Seek. Tom would hide; Paula would seek; and he would come up behind or under her until she rode his shoulders and he dumped her. Or she would hide; he would seek; and he would still manage to surprise her into a dunk. Another game consisted of her stepping on his hands; then he would fling her up and over backwards. The buoyancy of the water equalized their strengths enough for her to toss him about too, but, to his enjoyment, she seemed to get the worst of it. Alternately, she would turn outward; he would come up under her; her legs would stiffen, and with a powerful upward thrust he would catapult her off his hands out of the water and into a dive.

That is just what Paula was expecting when he caught her unawares, grabbed her ankles and jerked her down with such force that she took in too much water and began to splutter and gasp. When she came up heaving and in obvious distress, Tom flung her over his shoulder and gave her three hard whacks in the middle of her back with his free hand. Then he let her body slide down his and locked his arms and legs around her, cradling her until she coughed up all that she could.

He whispered apologetically, "I'm sorry. I'm so sorry," over and over again in her ear. "I don't know what I was thinking, throwing you around like a sack of potatoes. I should have been more gentle."

Paula wrestled from his grasp and shot him a steely look. "I am *not* a member of the opposite sex who needs to be coddled; I ask only to be treated equally. That shenanigan of yours was underhanded, and you, sir, are no sack of potatoes... so... neither am I!" She started coughing violently again and sank down into the water.

Tom pulled her up by her ponytail. "You are right... but I caused you distress, so it is up to me to relieve it." He cradled her in his arms again, and this time she did not resist.

When her breath started to come more easily, she opened her mouth to speak. He expected a tirade, but instead all she said was, "You play rough! You don't know your own strength."

"Again I'm so sorry. I don't know what got into me."

"Ten years of repressed emotion trying to get out—that's what's inside you. I just happened to be in the way," Paula spoke softly. "Thanks to you, and *no* thanks to you, I think I'll live, but I need to take a breather (no pun intended) for a few minutes."

Tom tipped her gently back onto the water, steadying her with his arm under her shoulders, afraid to let go of her again. He lay back too and they floated slowly with the undulating tide toward the path that would return them to solid, dry land. They saw fish-laden puffins flying home with supper and skua gulls circling above.

Paula spoke softly again. "You will be a better father to your children because of the time you spent playing on this island."

Chapter 7

In time the current brought them back to the rock. A lower tide made access more difficult; they would have to pull themselves up before they could gain good footing. Paula gave it a try. She could hold her weight, but she could not raise it. When Tom maneuvered to set her on his shoulders, she let out, "What are you doing! So help me, if you dunk me again...."

"I won't. I promise I won't. I'm still as sorry as I can be, but you've got to let me give you a boost, or you'll just hang there until you're food for the gulls."

Very smoothly and gently they rose out of the water until Paula steadied her feet on an outcropping and was able to advance. She wondered who would give Tom a boost, then remembered he could pull himself up; he had the strength of an ox. Soon he was right behind her, but he did not hurry her. The rocks were sharp, so they took their time.

Their shoes were a welcome sight. Tom warned her not to sit down to put them on, or she would have a black bottom inside and out. Paula leaned on his shoulders while he crouched to help her; he slid into his own with no problem. They walked slowly, arms around waists, back to their spot at the foot of the knoll.

By the time they arrived, Paula was shivering from the cool sea breeze against her wet body. Tom untied the blanket and she reached for her clothes. He took them away from her and grabbed his own sweatshirt, turning it inside out. Then he began to rub her harshly with it, all over. "If you put your clothes on now and they get wet too, you'll be freezing all afternoon. You need to let your body warm itself," and he continued to rub her down, tip to toe.

"What about you? Aren't *you* freezing?" Paula asked.

"I'm a hearty Irishman! I can take it! Grrr," he exclaimed in his best gorilla growl. He stopped massaging her upper thigh abruptly. "You have a scar here you didn't tell me about."

"Oh, that." She glanced where his hand paused. "That's my small pox vaccination. Surely you have one too."

"Just here, on my arm, as is usual."

She observed an almost invisible blemish at the base of his deltoid muscle. "For many girls my age, the upper thigh was used so as not to disfigure one's appearance. Who could have imagined the advent of the mini-skirt? Have you taken the polio vaccine?"

"Yes, polio vaccine."

"I lost a summer at the swimming pool during that epidemic. Braces?" and Paula smiled broadly to display the results of hers.

"No braces. Only my youngest sister." He resumed rubbing her briskly in an attempt to raise her body temperature.

He was right, of course. She did warm up. When he was satisfied that she would, he put her jacket around her shoulders, spread out the blanket and opened the picnic basket. Paula was almost as hungry as she had been cold. She was actually looking forward to a drink of warm stout. He used rocks as bottle openers, then handed her lunch. Boiled eggs, fresh garden carrots, bap and kipper were on the menu. Smoked herring was a first for Paula, but followed by a bite of roll and a swig, she managed just fine.

"Did you pack this? It just hits the spot."

"Hardly. My Aunt Moira did the honors."

"Thank her for me. She has put up with a lot, your being gone for so much of your visit," Paula asserted.

"Aunt Moira is a good sport. Her spies probably told her more than she needs to know, but she is always one for an intrigue. She won't be shy about telling me her mind. Just so long as she doesn't pass the word along to Mum.... That's why I thought to bring you out here—no spies."

They both admired the landscape, the contrast between sharp rocks and soft sand and grass, and the creatures that made this place home. A few clouds began to form in the west. "Better not rain," said Tom. "We're stuck here for the day 'til Des returns with the boat."

Paula feared she would not be starting out for Galway that day. She glanced at where her watch should have been and realized she left it in the locker with her ID. She depended on Tom to... and was suddenly aware that her thoughts betrayed a subtle change in her thinking. She *depended* on Tom to take care of things.

"This *is* such an idyllic place," she smiled. "Do you come here often?"

"Not really any more.... As a teen, you know, I came maybe two or three times during the summer. But this is the first time since my father's death.... The first time I've wanted to."

"Did you used to bring girls here?"

"Never. There was never anyone I wanted to share this with... until now. You're the first. You're the first I thought would be interested. The first I thought could take it. And was I wrong!" he joked. "You are such a ninny." She gave him a cross-eyed look and stuck out her chin in defiance.

"Do you date much? Do you have a steady girl?"

"Not likely," Tom declared. "You already know I won't be tying the knot for a long time. Dating here may not be what it is where you come from. Dating a steady girl is assumed a precursor to engagement and marriage. In school we do the group date sort of thing, but singling out a particular girl indicates an intent toward settling down. I'm not in a position to do that, as you know. And you. When did you start dating?"

"I think sixteen is an average age for single dating at home. Most date several people before they ever think about marriage."

"Have *you* dated several young men?"

"Of course."

"Did you 'go steady' with any?"

"More than one."

"And you didn't consider marriage with any of them?"

"Good heavens, no!"

"Then what's the point of going steady?"

"Frankly, I don't know." Paula looked puzzled. "It's a status symbol. It gives you a partner; someone you can count on in social situations—a kind of false security."

"What's the longest you've ever gone steady?" he asked.

"Two years. I was with my last boyfriend for two years."

"Two years! That's longer than most formal engagements! What happened?"

"I'm not willing to talk about it. I'm going to finish eating," Paula stated matter-of-factly.

"You did bring it up, you know."

"I know. And I'm not willing to talk about it; I'm going to finish eating." Tom could tell no further discussion would ensue.

Together they finished every last bite his aunt packed. "Hold out your hands, here, over the grass," he directed and poured the last of the ale over hers and his own. "Now rub them together briskly. The alcohol will cut the fish oil so you won't smell like puffin food all afternoon. Here, wipe them on the edge of the blanket." He was right, of course. Her hands now smelled of stout instead of fish.

"Warm now?" When she nodded, Tom sat down behind her and removed her jacket. "Good. Because I'm going to do something I've been wanting to for the last two days."

Paula stiffened but told herself that she would not "assume" the worst again. "What's that?" She tried to sound casual.

"I'm going to lose myself in your hair." And he broke the bright band on her ponytail to let her hair cascade down her back. Paula did not know if she should protest—so she did not. Tom used his fingers as a comb gently running them through her saltwater tangles.

"Is this a service big brothers usually render to their sisters?" she pried.

"No, it's a privilege known only to lovers."

"And how would *you* know?" she taunted.

"I'm not willing to talk about it," he replied smugly.

Gone was the big brother Tom had claimed to be. The man who replaced him was thoughtful, playful, considerate... and was beginning to take liberties with their familiarity. "Your hair is beautiful. Why do you keep it wound up so tight?"

"Convenience. A defensive masquerade. Why are you so interested?"

"I don't know. Because it's one of the few attributes of a girl we guys are allowed to admire, I suppose. We certainly can't comment publicly on a figure, or the softness of skin, or where she has stripes." He gave her suit top a snap. "Not in public at least. There's definitely no touching below the shoulders! We're pretty much stuck with what's above—which is very, very appealing, by the way." He gave her shoulder a little nip and continued gently working his way through her snarls. "That's why dancing is so popular among us young folks; it affords us a casual intimacy."

She shifted and broached another sensitive subject. "Do you think marriage is a right, a privilege, an obligation or a sentence?"

"Hmmm. That's a hard one. What makes you ask?"

"Our experiences with displaying affection and dating are so different, I wonder how you view marriage."

"In that context, I guess marriage is an obligation. It is a means to maintain the family bloodline and establish the legitimacy of children and their rights of inheritance. A man's first job is his home and family. Anything else he does is a means to fulfill that obligation," Tom asserted. "You?"

"I think of marriage as a privilege—a privilege to have another person love you enough to want to share the rest of his life with you. Does affection play *any* part in your view of marriage?" she asked.

"I would expect mutual affection and admiration to go without saying," he stated.

"But the obligation to marry supercedes finding an ideal partner?"

"Put that way, I suppose so. But I don't believe *you* wouldn't feel a sense of obligation to support the person you love and the institution of marriage. At least neither of us thinks marriage is a sentence," he declared.

"What about the woman who finds herself with 9—12—14 children and another on the way and whose husband spends his nights at the pub? With no possibility of working to help support her family and lift them out of poverty or with no means to limit the size of her family, is that not a sentence? I doubt she thinks much of bloodline and rights of inheritance," Paula claimed.

"She's not going to be thinking about love nor affection either."

"What about parenthood? Is parenthood a right, a privilege, an obligation or a sentence?" She continued her questioning.

"That's an obligation too. It is one's duty to be the best parent possible to one's children, to provide for their needs."

"I see parenthood as a privilege—a privilege to help shape lives, to guide growth," she offered. "How about having children? Is that a right, a privilege, an obligation or a sentence?"

"It's the same thing."

"No. Having children and being a parent are two *different* things," Paula corrected. "Having children is creating life; parenting is taking care of the life you've created."

"Well then, having children would be one of the obligations of marriage, sustaining the bloodline." He paused. "I'm going to guess. You see it as a privilege."

"If one *wanted* children and biology made it possible, then yes, it would be a privilege to foster new life."

"We can scratch 'right' and 'sentence' off your list, but we come down evenly divided on 'privilege' and 'obligation.' What do you think that means?" Tom was afraid to ask.

"It means that even though we speak the same language, we don't speak the same language at all," she confirmed. "I'm not sure I've met anyone so diametrically opposed to my way of thinking. Do your opinions come from reasoning or from teachings?"

"What I express here is what I have been taught, but I also believe it is true and correct. The teachings of the Church provide stability within our society."

"What is your position on contraception?" Paula asked fearlessly.

"The same as the Church's. It is unthinkable, a mortal sin. Birth control should not be made commonly available."

"But it's the common woman who suffers most because it is not available to her," and in her best Walter Cronkite voice, she mimicked, "National Network TV here taking a survey on a current controversial topic. Mr. O'Connell, what method of contraception do *you* find most effective?"

Tom was astonished at her audacity and began to stammer a reply.

"Mr. O'Connell, is your embarrassment because you *do* know or you *don't* know to what I am referring?"

Tom was still speechless. "Whew! You're good at that. Do you want a job in Belfast?"

"What method *do* you use? I can't believe you abstain."

"I'm too much of a hot-blooded Irishman for that!"

"Did you ever beget a child without 'benefit of clergy?'" Paula shocked him with the boldness of her question.

"Not that I've been told!"

"So you do admit that you've...."

Tom's face flushed. "I'm a hot-blooded Irishman, Paula, who's not likely to marry for another ten years. What do you expect?"

"I expect any young man your age to know what to do to prevent conception outside of marriage. Do your sisters use The Pill?"

"How would I ever know?"

"As head of the family, you should make it your business to know."

His stammered as he asked, "Do... you? Use... The Pill?"

"Having lived with a man for two years, do you doubt it? I'm not so naïve as to think that getting pregnant is a gift from the Almighty. I don't want the course of my life changed forever by accident, by deceit or by force. That's why I plan trips to London periodically where contraceptives are readily available. My family supports that I do." Anticipating his reply, she stated, "I suppose you're anti-abortion too."

"The Church is very explicit. Abortion is unthinkable, a mortal sin; it interferes with God's plan. Abortion should never be legalized for it would lead to indiscriminate killing."

"Do you deny that abortion occurs now?" Paula challenged.

"Of course it occurs; there is a terrible stigma placed on unwed mothers, for illegitimates can't inherit. But there is more shipping off of young girls to have their babes and give them up for adoption than there is actual abortion."

"For poor as well as rich? What about those who don't have the means to be 'shipped off?' Are the babies taken in as little brothers and sisters or are they doomed to a life of shame? And what does that say about one's 'obligation' to provide for children?" Paula interrogated.

"There are ways. Jumping down stairs. Taking hot baths. There are older women who know what to do, who can give girls...."

"Abortive 'teas?'" Paula interrupted sharply.

He did not reply to her acerbic remark.

"Tom, whose responsibility is it to take care of an unwanted pregnancy?"

"If it's a woman's design or her business, if she derives income for her favors, then it's the woman's responsibility."

"What if it's not a business. What if it's accidental, with someone you care for?"

"I would never let that happen!" Tom finished with her hair and turned her to face him. He reached for one of the few ground flowers hiding among the grasses, plucked it and tucked it behind her ear saying, "One more flower for my fiercely independent flower child."

"You're the only one who ever dared to put flowers in my hair," she confessed.

"You see, I'm not so conservative as you make me out to be," he professed. "But I can see now why we're fighting the influx of your liberal western ideas. Your talk of 'free love,' anti-this and civil-that, contraception and abortion, testing all the limits.... Your uncompromising idealism and feminist politics are threatening our cultural and religious values. If an act is morally or ethically wrong, and then the civil law changes, that doesn't change the morality of the act. It simply changes the consequences of your decisions in the eyes of the law—not in the eyes of God. Making your own choices comes with huge responsibility, Paula. Accepted teachings provide structure and stability."

"Your attitude is so 19th Century," she cajoled, trying to temper his seriousness.

"My attitude is not 19th Century; it is far older than that," Tom argued. "*My attitude* assures stability. *My attitude* assures continuity. *My attitude* assures fidelity." He flipped her over onto her stomach and firmly, but not harshly, held her there with his knee. "And this particular *attitude* of *yours* is one I admire *very* much!" He began to massage her back and limbs, removing every blade of grass and speck of grit along the way.

* * * * *

Their verbal sparring left Paula limp, but she did not bid him stop. She tingled at the touch of his tracing finger around her back. "What are you doing?"

"I'm drawing a map of Ireland for you. I want embedded in your memory every place you'll see here." Tom outlined the fairly straight east and southern coasts, the many inlets and bays which cut into the west, and the river Shannon flowing from the north. He sketched Valentia and Puffin Islands, and with light strokes, he painted in the North Atlantic Ocean and Irish Sea.

He wanted to know her route, and as Paula told him, he marked each locale with his thumb. "I took the Holyhead Ferry to Dublin. I've been through Kildare, Tipperary and Cork, Limerick and County Kerry to the famous Valentia Island and the fantastical Puffin Island. I shall continue through Galway, Sligo and Donegal to Londonderry and Belfast in the north where I'll take a ferry to Scotland."

"That's a lot of ground to cover."

"Your whole country is less than a third the area of Colorado. At home it would be barely a day's drive."

"You don't have to go to Scotland, you know," he suggested.

"I know.... But I will," she affirmed. "If Ireland is an island, why do you refer to it as the mainland when on Valentia Island?"

"Because it's too cumbersome to say 'main island.'" Tom lay back near her, drinking in the sun himself.

"I admit, there is reassurance and comfort in your way of thinking, stability in realizing answers before questions are even asked. I understand the security a woman would feel in knowing she'd be honored and admired, if not truly loved, for the duration of a marriage as long as she fulfilled her wifely duties," she thought aloud.

Sensing his guard down, she jumped atop him, straddled his waist and pinned his arms to the ground. "Now it's *my* turn," Paula dared. "*You* shall be *my* canvas. I'm taking you to all the places I've been."

Tom's broad chest gave her an expanse to work with. She slid to his side. He was startled when her hand crept below his waistband. "Where do you think you're going?"

"First stop was Tangiers," she teased. Paula sketched a route north along the Mediterranean coast of his ribs from Valencia and Barcelona to Marseilles and Genoa, turned south to Rome and Naples, then north through Venice and Florence and over the Alps to Austria, Switzerland and Germany. She crisscrossed his sternum from Munich to Normandy to East Berlin and back. She kept returning to Paris; it was her center. The strikes there forced her south and west into Spain again and Portugal, then back to Paris. She followed his collarbone from Belgium to Amsterdam and Copenhagen, trailing up the length of his neck to Scandinavia. She traced his chiseled jaw through Norway and Sweden, even touching the ear lobe of Finland long enough to get a stamp in her passport. She crossed the Arctic Circle for a second time and descended Sweden bound for Paris again. She etched her way from Paris to London and then settled into the hollow beneath his shoulder in Ireland.

When Paula's journey ended on Puffin Island, Tom pulled her down close to him, and her head lay in France for a very long time.

He roused her from her snooze. "Are we really so different? Seriously." He stroked her hair away from her face while she pondered.

"You've developed your social view from teachings, from someone else's ideal of how things should be. Mine is from discovery, observing what works for others and selecting what I think will work for me. You have history behind you; I'm pushing limits on the present. Which belief system will prove to be a stronger foundation for this changing future in front of us remains to be seen."

"An Irishman has two sides—the side you see and the one you don't see—just like a coin," Tom murmured.

"And that's how you see the world too, as black or white, right or wrong, sin or virtue, with no room for the influence of emotion or reason, the same code for everyone. I see sin and virtue on a sliding scale, and I'm trying to find a 'mean,' a morality between the two that I can live with as long as it doesn't bring harm to anyone else. I accept that it will not be the same for everyone. I probably let my feelings wield too much influence over reason right now, but I hope I'll mellow over time." Paula grew thoughtful.

"I don't deal in absolutes," she continued. "You do. For instance, you believe that abortion is wrong, absolutely. I believe that there may be a time when it is the prudent course of action. I hope I am never faced with having to make that decision, but I reserve the right of self-determination."

"Are you not religious? Do you not fear the wrath of God?" Tom prodded.

"If you are asking if I follow the prescripts of a specific Christian religion, I would have to say I'm more spiritual than religious." Paula reflected, "Religion has no monopoly on morality. Most people behave morally most of the time. They care about the consequences of their actions and they recognize the boundary between what's appropriate and inappropriate. I believe in a God who has given us free will for a reason—to find that morality. What is the purpose of free will if not to use it? Decision-making is evaluating alternatives. Decisions should be made with a clear understanding of why they might be *right* rather than the fear they might be *wrong*. Living by a prescription for doing God's will is living with fear—a fear that we'll never be able to live up to His will for us.

"The difference between the two of us, Tom, is whether we choose to live with hope or live with fear. 'Conscience is but a word that cowards use.' You quoted that yourself. If we exercise free will in our choices wisely, we should be led to a path parallel to what you would call God's path for us. My fear is not God's 'wrath,' His judgement of man... but how *man* judges his fellow man, often in God's name. Prejudice, hatred and intolerance have to be taught. They are not innate in us; they are a choice we make. We all have the potential for being virtuous. A virtuous person makes the right choices regularly, over and over, but being human, not necessarily every single time. We should do the good we can and live our lives with purpose and love while trying to make the world a better place... each in his own small way.

"This is what I believe, but I have no idea if it is a formal teaching of any organized religion," Paula finished.

"I know what I've been taught to believe," Tom asserted. "Lust is a sin. Sex outside marriage is a sin. Sex within marriage is for the purpose of procreation, is not to be interfered with in any way, and is not necessarily for pleasure. Life, once created, is sacred. I don't think having more sexual freedom would make me happier. I try to live within the code I've been handed."

"But you also have a means of reconciling what you do that absolves you of torment after the fact," Paula reminded him. "I try to eliminate guilt from the equation by reasoning before the fact. The game-changing realities of sexual freedom, birth control, abortion and alternative lifestyles are not the only moral questions we'll face in our lifetimes. They're just the first of many."

"I'm certain about what's wrong; I just don't know what's right," Tom confessed.

"And I've had such limited life experience, I don't know what's right either," Paula admitted.

"Do we have *anything* in common?" he asked.

"Not really. Not much of substance anyway. We do both have a curiosity for the new and different. We hunger for intellectual stimulation. We're educated, and we enjoy music and dance. You are confident enough to doubt, and I am open enough to consider. We both have a dash of poetry and adventure in our souls. But in the broader spectrum of life-issues, we really don't." Paula's hand danced around Italy. "I hope we share a mutual affection and regard."

"For the first time today, I think we agree," Tom smiled weakly. "It *has* become apparent we have very little in common. But that's the point—the allure. We aren't carbon copies. We don't march to the same drummer. We expand each other's experience. You represent the dreams I dare to dream. And I, the stability you seek... whether you realize it yet or not." He tilted her chin upward to lock her gaze. "Paula? Could we ever be... compatible?"

"In what way?"

"All ways."

"It's obvious that our views of the roles of men and women in society and in marriage are *in*compatible, so practically speaking, it is doubtful we could ever find harmony. Mentally, we seem to be well attuned; we can each take as well as give. Emotionally, I think we're closer than it would appear. You're beginning to let go your reticence and I'm trying not to be so outspoken."

"And physically?" Tom asked.

Paula did not hesitate to answer. "Absolutely. No doubt."

The electricity in their verbal intercourse aroused them both. If Tom's soul were conflicted, he did not betray that emotion. He simply enveloped Paula completely with his body and would not let her go.

Chapter 8

The sound of a horn signaled the return of Des and his boat. Reluctantly, they slipped back into their clothes, packed up the basket, and wrapped the blanket around both sets of shoulders. As they walked slowly, hand in hand to the edge of the cliff and their departure, Paula asked, "Tom, how will you ever reconcile your beliefs with everything we've said and done today?"

"I'm not even going to try."

He looped and tied the ends of the blanket again and they chained themselves as before. She descended the graded slope first but not before she memorized the scene of puffins and rabbits who seemed delighted to have their island back The rabbits were carefree, darting in and out of burrows and among rocks, curiously searching for new ways to familiar places. The puffins huddled together in pairs as examples of their sexual fidelity and the sharing of responsibilities in lasting partnerships. She envied them both for their freedom to live in harmony as nature intended.

The boat was lower than when they disembarked that morning—the work of tides, she supposed. Paula climbed down as close as she could, maybe eight feet above the boat, and then turned around. Tom was just behind her and threw the basket into the small vessel. He removed the blanket from their wrists and let it drop too. "It's too far now. I can't hang onto you any longer, but you'll do fine. When you jump, timing is more important than distance. Wait until the boat just begins to ride the crest of a wave, and then remember to jump out, not down. Des will catch you. Do you need a push?"

Paula shook her head. She did not need a push; she needed a ladder... and some courage would be nice too. She heard the two men yell, "Jump!" and she did, landing hard against Des who pulled her away from the rail. There was a thud, and Tom was by her side.

Des headed the boat north and west and sped toward Valentia. Considering she was not drowned, knocked senseless, impaled or ravaged, she decided that her adventure was very worthwhile. Tom hugged her close to his chest—to keep her warm, he said. She watched over his shoulder as Puffin Island disappeared. No one would believe her day. She was not sure *she* did. She doubted any "ride" could top this one.

* * * * *

Their boat moved into the harbor slowly, past the lighthouse and into a slip near the clock tower. Most vessels were already back in so the docks were crowded. The two adventurers thanked Des again for rescuing them from the ferocious wildlife and the inhospitable cliffs. Aware that they had returned to civilization with all its spies, Paula was careful to keep her hands in her jacket pockets when she turned to say goodbye. "This has been the greatest day! Thank you so much for sharing your private island with me."

"I wouldn't have shared it with anyone else. You are the perfect partner in my imaginary world." Then, with a grin, he added, "But this great day is not over yet. You're coming with me."

She began to protest, "I have packing to do. I need to clean up and change."

"No.... You don't.... I'm not going to let you out of my sight. I'm afraid you're a figment of my imagination and I don't dare let go of you lest you evaporate." They both understood now the rules discouraging their public displays, but Tom paid no mind and pulled her next to him until they each wove an arm behind the other. She placed her head on his shoulder and he planted kisses in her hair. Oblivious of the eyes in the village, they made their way, in step, along the path and into town.

They stopped by his car to deposit the blanket and basket. This night they patronized Dunbar's, a place sporting less wood, a more subdued proprietor and a smaller crowd than they rubbed elbows with the previous evening. A few familiar faces greeted them, including the American hostlers.

"We have to make an appearance at each establishment. We cannot play favorites; we must spread our good fortune around," Tom explained, almost apologizing for the lack of ambiance. He settled them side-by-side at a table in a remote corner of the dining area, and miraculously as before their drinks of choice appeared.

After an initial toast, Paula got up to excuse herself. "Where do you think you're going?" Tom objected.

"I've got to clean up before I face a plate of food."

"Then, let me escort you," and he rose as well.

"It really isn't necessary. I think I can find my way."

"I want to make sure you don't find your way out the door!" Tom kidded and accompanied her back across the room.

Paula took her time washing her face and hands and the other parts of her body that she could reach discreetly. She jiggled as much sand out of her clothes and swimsuit as she dared leave on the floor and then tried to whisk the heaps around with a towel. She tamed the wild in her hair and thought to discard the now limp wildflower but did not. When she was as presentable as a few minutes could make her, she left the room and found Tom waiting right outside the door.

"Thank you for keeping my flower" was all he said as he led her back to their table. Their supper was waiting, hot and hearty Irish Stew and brown bread, and they attacked it hungrily. He took care of it all, of course. As nice as it was not to think for herself for a while, Paula wondered why that should be.

Sitting beside her, Tom was possessive in a protective sort of way. When his arm was not around her back or shoulders, his hand was holding hers, and he leaned in close when they spoke. She shook her head. "I don't understand why you had to accompany me across the room. I'm not going to bolt on you. I'll at least say goodbye before I do."

"It was a symbol, a sign to everyone here that you are taken. You are not free to be approached. We are a couple, and the other men must respect that and stand away."

She could not believe he was serious. "You didn't do that last night."

"Last night you were allowed to talk and dance with other fellows... within limits. Tonight you are mine!"

"Allowed?" Paula glared at him.

"Mine, absolutely!" Tom glared back, half in jest, and tightened his hold on her.

She bristled. "I am *not* your possession... a souvenir from your holiday... another symbol of your latent adolescent rebellion like your car or your boat. You cannot foster a relationship with an object!"

Her sharp retort surprised Tom. Now that he was an adult, not even his mother would rebuke him like that. She would have referred his insolence to his father. But he had to admit Paula probably had cause; twice that day he objectified her. He touched a nerve and made a mental note not to dehumanize her again.

When he relaxed his hold, she asked calmly, "Which side of the Irishman coin am I witnessing now?"

"The I've-still-got-a-lot-to-learn side, and I'm so glad I have you for a teacher. We'd better eat up and get out of here before I embarrass myself further and create more tales for wagging tongues."

They finished their stew soaking up every last bit of sauce with bread. Steaming cups were set before them. "What potion have you concocted now?" Paula shook her head.

"No more sudsy brew for you tonight. We have serious business ahead and you must be at the top of your game. This is Irish Coffee, guaranteed to warm you from the tip of your nose to the tips of your tan-striped toes, and put you under my spell."

"I've been under every other part of your body today, I might as well be under your spell too," Paula joked.

Tom flushed a beet red behind his grin and hoped none of the other patrons heard her. She took a sip of her coffee and blurted out, "Good Lord, this is strong!"

"The better to seduce you with, my dear."

They finished and left as before, with no order, no bill and no money changing hands except with the owner at the end of the bar after handshakes and thanks all around.

* * * * *

Tom drove them a few kilometers along the western coast of the island to a spot that had real sand on a real beach—no grass, birds or rabbits. He had piled firewood nearby and set a small fire. He must have been a scout in a previous life for the fire took right away and added a pleasant warmth to the darkness descending around them. Paula wiggled her toes deep down into the sand and recalled other beaches where she had done the same. The same stars and the same moon were fixed in their familiar places. Valentia Island compared very favorably.

Tom approached. "Enjoying this?"

"Very much. This is a wonderful farewell surprise."

"There's more." He took her hands and placed them over her eyes. "Keep them closed 'til I get back."

Paula heard him walk away, the car door open and then close again. "Oh, great," she thought. "Stranded on an island. Stranded on a beach. What else could possibly happen today?" She heard footsteps returning and hoped they were his.

"Open." And when she did, Tom held out before her a guitar, not a new guitar but a very well loved one.

"Where did you ever get this?" she asked, surprised.

"O'Hanlon's. I borrowed it," Tom revealed proudly. "No music on Sunday nights."

"And what are *we* going to do with this?"

"*You* are going to play and sing, just as you did when you *weren't* a Hippie."

"Isn't it sinful to play and sing on Sunday?"

"Not if *you* do it, you heretic!"

"You've really scripted this, haven't you?"

"That's my job. A good production requires careful planning and attention to detail," he boasted.

"What if I were to 'rebel' and refuse to play the role you've written for me?"

"You won't."

"How can you be so sure?"

"Because you're enjoying this as much as I am," he smiled.

"Pretty stiff payback, making me sing for my supper. You're not expecting me to play the flute or the tambourine too are you?"

Tom laughed. "No. We'll save those for another time."

"Will you pull a piano out of your pocket and do your part here, or is this going to be a solo performance?" Paula turned her face toward the sky, summoning courage.

"You'll be pretty much on your own tonight."

Resolved to her fate, she shook her head. "My playing will be nothing like we heard last night. I haven't touched a guitar since the trip over on the freighter, and I don't do rock so you'll have to settle for folk... but I'll agree to a short set as long as you're willing to join in when you know the song."

"Right," was all Tom said as he laid out a couple of logs to the side of the fire for her. She sat cross-legged on them, rested the guitar on her right thigh, ran her left hand along its neck and plucked the strings. No tuning was necessary. She fingered a *G*-chord. Tom also sat cross-legged opposite her in the sand, anticipation breaking through his smile.

"This first is a really old American mountain folk song which tells a story—just so you have something to compare with the protest songs coming up." Thankful for that cup of Irish Coffee, she hoped her ease would soon follow. She launched into a lively version of "Fox Went Out on a Chilly Night" and could tell that he was enjoying the fruits of his surprise.

"Every culture has its own brand of folk music, and we Americans borrow from the best. Here's one we've taken from you." Paula began "Cockles and Mussels" and gave Tom a hard stare when time came for the chorus. He did, reluctantly, join in.

"Everybody knows 'Michael, Row the Boat Ashore,'" and she coaxed another chorus out of him. Then followed others Tom knew: "Greensleeves," "Scarborough Fair," "Scarlet Ribbons," and "Amazing Grace," and he became more comfortable adding his voice to hers.

They heard applause coming from behind them on the walking path. "Very nice, Mr. Thomas. Very nice. Will ye be takin' yer show to the pub anytime soon?"

"Not likely, James." Tom laughed with embarrassment. Spies, he thought.

Protest and message songs, those most frequently requested at rallies, Paula sang with an understanding of one who had been there: "Mary, Don't You Weep," "Where Have All the Flowers Gone?" "What Have They Done to the Rain?" "This Land is Your Land," "If I had a Hammer," and "Blowin' in the Wind." Tom was moved by the emotion she could not hide. He had not heard most of them before.

She added "Are You Going to San Francisco?" (featuring the flower he had laced in her hair, to Tom's delight) and "Go Where You Wanna Go" from the Mamas & Papas. She tried to mimic Janis Joplin's song of freedom. Even though Tom had not heard or seen the psychedelic rock singer perform, he could tell that Paula's impersonation was pretty poor. They laughed together at her feeble attempt.

"That's what these groups, all the counter-culture kids, are searching for—just as we are with our personal lives—searching for an alternative to what came before and for a reality that makes sense. We're all learning to be adults, to find our own identities, and we'd like the world to come together," Paula mused. Now she was the one who became introspective. "I have not earned the right to sing these songs. I do not have the courage of some, to be jailed for my convictions."

Tom left her with her thoughts to tend the fire. Then he squeezed behind her on the logs. This time his head rested on her shoulder as they sang an old song from his culture and one from hers: "Too-Ra-Loo-Ra-Loo-Ral (That's an Irish Lullaby)" and "We Shall Overcome." They found a harmony together that pleased them both.

When she was all strummed out, Paula put the guitar down, turned to Tom and said, "Your turn. I expect at least 'Danny Boy.'" He stood sheepishly before her and obliged. Underneath all that bluff and bluster there was a beautiful Irish tenor voice which hit the high notes true and with a confidence born of practice.

"That was positively beautiful. Is there anything you *can't* do?" she asked, still in awe of his performance.

"I can't play guitar.... I can't stop time.... I can't convince you that we'd make a very good pair... but I'm not about to give up trying!"

As the fire died down, their singing gave way to dancing. They made their own music with soft choruses from their favorites. Tom took the lead.

"This is surreal; it cannot be happening," Paula whispered. "If this were a novel or a film, it would be a fantasy. I feel like a star in a remake of every summer romance movie: being rescued by a knight in shining armor, dancing Irish jigs, frolicking on a deserted island, swimming with the fishes, singing and dancing on a beach in the arms of a handsome stranger. When will we see 'The End?'"

"Perhaps we won't."

* * * * *

Tom could sense Paula's increasing exhaustion; her body leaned more and more heavily against his and her feet moved slowly, if at all. He sat her down while he took the guitar back to his car to "get it out of the damp." He returned with the blanket, their day's faithful companion and lifeline, and spread it out near her. She crawled over to join him and rolled on her back looking at the stars. He lay beside her doing the same. "Well," he began. "Have I passed your test?"

"What test is that?"

"The brooding/introspective/repressed versus the thoughtful/confident/fun-loving Irishman test."

"A+ all the way. I haven't had such a good time since... I can't remember when."

"And how do your words taste?"

"Like seaweed mixed with black sand. I admit that I was so very wrong to assume you were anything other than perfect. I apologize for my remarks and ask that you forget I ever spoke those words," Paula offered feigned concern.

"Apology accepted. Now, wash them down with this," and Tom handed her a mug of hot tea from a thermos that mysteriously appeared.

"You really have thought of everything, haven't you?"

"Everything but how to make this evening last forever." He hesitated before continuing. "I cannot bear to think of you at the 'Festival of the Flower Children' amongst thousands of people sharing a blanket with someone else."

"You sound jealous." Paula tweaked his ribs. "I know how to take care of myself. Maybe I'll meet another gentleman just like you. In reality, I'll probably be the only one there who isn't tripped out on acid and who actually listens to the music."

"Look at you now," Tom scolded. "We've barely been out for a day and you're limp as a rag. You're bound to fall asleep sometime in that two days and a stranger might come along and take advantage of you. I don't want...."

"If you're so worried, meet me there. Justify a trip to London as background info for a documentary piece."

"That won't fly. I'm already scheduled for Belfast then. You could return to Dublin after... to let me know you're all right," Tom dared to suggest.

"I'll send a postcard. It's cheaper."

"After Woburn where will you go?" he asked.

"Back to Paris... to make arrangements for fall semester. I need to settle someplace for the winter. Hitchhiking in cold weather is too gruesome. I intend to enroll in one of the universities there, if they'll take me. I want an educational experience that is really demanding, something I have to work hard at to succeed. I haven't been challenged like that yet, and I think it would be good practice for grad school. I figure no matter what the classes are, if they are in a foreign language that will be challenge enough."

"So you speak French?" Tom inquired.

"Some."

"Anything else?"

"Some German. You?" Paula asked.

"Irish Gaelic, of course. And Latin."

"Ah, that classical education."

"After Paris, could you return to Dublin?" Tom suggested again.

"I'm already locked in to an international work camp for six weeks. I'll be in southern France with a group of about thirty students from all over Europe who have volunteered to do restoration work. Opportunities are developing throughout the continent for young people from different countries and backgrounds to come together, to live and work together in peace and harmony so they'll go home and spread the word. I think it will be good practice for the Peace Corps, if that's in my future."

"Do you get paid for this?"

"Oh no. It's strictly volunteer. In exchange for hard manual labor, we'll get room and board and intercultural exchange. It's all very altruistic."

"Sounds like a forced labor camp to me. Is this supposed to change the world?" Tom asked cynically.

"For each in his own small way. This will be an opportunity to break down some of the stereotypes we all have of other cultures. You and I know how that works! I think it will have greater impact than marching with a placard."

"Now I have visions of you sharing a blanket with someone in the south of France too. I can't stand this!"

"You'd better get over it. Jealousy is one of the seven deadly sins, you know."

"Yes, I do know my sins, very well: envy, lust, anger, pride, sloth, gluttony, and covetousness. Technically it's envy, not jealousy, but they feel the same. And I'm about as deep into most of them right now as I have ever been. Here I am lying out in front of God and everybody doing things I shouldn't be doing, thinking thoughts I shouldn't be thinking and expressing doubt in my faith; yet I'm feeling no shame, no guilt, no fear. Why is that?" Tom asked himself aloud.

"My answer would be, because you have done nothing wrong, nothing for which you should feel shameful or guilty or fearful. Desire and pleasure are not sins. Your answer would have to do with delayed reaction. You are too close to your supposed sinful acts to realize their consequences yet." Paula's tone turned sarcastic. "*I* am the villain in this story. *I'm* the corrupting influence, the one who has brought censored material into your life and lured you to sinful words and deeds. *You* are the innocent victim. That should buy you some mercy."

"You're tired and you're talking nonsense. Sit up and have more tea." Tom had some too. "Now, come here." They lay back together on the blanket where she fit herself naturally and comfortably against the curves of his body.

After a time, he whispered, "Come away with me to Dublin, Paula."

"What?"

"This isn't the alcohol talking tonight. I'm serious. Tomorrow. Come away with me to Dublin."

"What do you propose we *do* in Dublin?" she answered just as seriously.

"Be happy. Be complete. Feel free... the same freedom I'm feeling now... that I've felt these last three wonderful days with you."

"Sounds tempting, if not impossible. What would you do with me? Hide me on your sailboat? Do you propose I become a kept woman? We couldn't continue like this in public," she reminded him.

"I admit I haven't thought it out yet, but we have the drive back to come up with a plan. I know you see vast differences between us, but you said yourself you are up for a challenge and what greater challenge could there be than taking on the Catholic Church and all of Ireland?"

Despite the gravity of the conversation, Paula had to laugh. "Oh, Tom. There is so much in you that's endearing. *You* know that if we were anywhere else in the world, we wouldn't be doing this. Frankly, we probably wouldn't have met at all were we anyplace but this isolated island village on the west coast of Ireland."

Fixing her stare on Polaris, Paula continued, undaunted. "If we were discovered on St. Stephen's Green wrapped around each other as we have been, we would be tarred and feathered. There's an element of providence working in our favor here because we aren't that somewhere else. We've been granted a reprieve from censure. We feel we're in a safe place—a cocoon."

She snuggled her head in the hollow that was Ireland. "But in Dublin, we never would have associated in the first place. In Dublin, I would be shunned for such behavior, and I don't know to what hell your family would condemn you. You need time... time and distance... to find a comfortable place between what you believe and what you've been taught. My going with you to Dublin tomorrow is not an option."

"The fact that I'm an Irish Catholic man lying here with a woman allowing her to tell me what's what... is remarkable. Today you reached down my throat, grabbed my repression, pulled it out by its roots, cast it away and let it sink to the bottom of the sea. And my guilt has gone with it. I thank you for that."

He wove his fingers between hers. "You've had your turn; now *I'm* going to tell *you* what's what. The time will come, Miss Paula, when you'll have to finally make hard choices for yourself, decide what *you* believe. Whether or not you have the help of a religion, family, conscience, you'll have to come down on one side or the other of every important issue facing both of us. You cannot wander indefinitely, either in body or mind."

He rolled toward her and bent his elbow to perch his head on his hand. His slate blue eyes bore deeply into hers. He placed his other hand on her face, laced his fingers into her hair and punctuated each statement with his thumb tracing across her cheekbone.

"I *know* what I've been taught. I *know* what I believe. I believe we ultimately want the same: home, family, stability, purpose, fulfillment. I believe we can find these together. I believe I can give you the stability you know, deep down, you are seeking. I believe I can help you find the purpose and fulfillment you want. I believe you can give me the home and family and purpose I search for."

Tom put his hand across Paula's mouth to hush her protests. "I know what you're going to say. 'Not now. Not yet.' But I ask *why* not now; *why* not yet? You said yourself, we have the power to change the world—each in his own small way. Let's try to change this crazy world of ours together, hand-in-hand, for everyone to see."

Paula tried to stop the tear that slid onto his hand and pooled beneath his fingers. "You know as well as I that as soon as we leave Valentia Island, this magical spell surrounding us will be broken.

We'll be thrust into your world which lacks tolerance and into mine which demands it. I want to cherish this as a beautiful memory, not watch it disintegrate in the realities imposed by the outside world."

Tom kissed her forehead. "Let me hold you tight, then, and dream of your never going away."

The two passed several minutes in silence, each one lost in his own regrets. Paula startled suddenly, "What time is it? It must be near eleven. We need to go. I'll be locked out and you'll miss the ferry!"

"No matter," Tom whispered as he folded her to his chest and cocooned them tightly together in his blanket. "We'll make a home together under the stars."

Her hair spread out as a pillow for them both. "Can you keep us awake?" she appealed. "I don't want to waste a minute of this night with sleep."

"I'll try." He covered her face with kisses. "Come to Dublin?" She shook her head but returned his favor. "How far *are* you willing to go with me?" he coaxed.

"As far as the turnoff to Galway."

"You aren't listening. How far are you willing to go with me?"

Gleaning his intent, she asked, "How far dare you?"

"How far will you let me?"

He found his answer in her smile.

Paula rarely invoked pleas to the Almighty, but she felt herself asking for strength. "Please, help us both stay safe and sane."

They finally did fall asleep, reluctantly, with Paula's head nestled somewhere east of Denmark and Tom's hand swimming the Irish Sea. The last words she heard were a resumption of the previous night's lament. "Conscience holds me back no longer; courage only makes me stronger, /Strong enough to let you know I care for you, so please don't go... from my life. / If you should choose to leave, it seems, you'll truly trample on my dreams."

Hardly Yeats, Paula mused, but Tom's attempts at verse were a valiant effort and endearing nonetheless. Welcome, poetic dreamer!

* * * * *

Paula awoke to the third sunny sky in as many days. She and Tom were still rolled together in his blanket, so she took a quick inventory with her one hand that was not interlocked with his body. Her clothes were shed hours ago. She was relieved to feel her swim suit still in place and intact, however. He had evidently practiced restraint; she was not sure she could have. Good thing he was the one in control.

It was then Paula noticed Tom noticing her. He brushed her hair away from her face and kissed her smile. "Welcome to this day, my flower child," he said pulling what was left of a very bedraggled posy from her hair.

"You're showing introspection again, staring at me like that." She blinked the sleep from her eyes.

"I was just imagining how it would feel to wake up to you like this every morning. Sleep well?" he asked, as his hand found its way over her shoulder and down her back.

"About as well as you did, I suppose. So tell me, how many of the seven deadly sins have you *now* committed?"

"No more than before. The way to Heaven is still open for this repentant sinner, no matter how unrepentant he may secretly be," Tom reassured her, a smile escaping his lips.

Paula hesitated to ask. "Any regrets?"

"Only that I cannot convince you to come with me."

"Not now. Not yet," she said shaking her head.

"There's nothing that would make you change your mind? Alter your plans?"

"If my brother got his draft notice, then I would be gone in a flash to see him before he shipped out. Other than that, I'm determined to stick with my plan. I *have* to leave today, and I'm going north," she insisted.

"You're *obliged* to?"

"I *intend* to," she emphasized, leaving no doubt in Tom's mind.

"Remember, you said you'd send a postcard after Woburn... to let me know you survived unscathed."

Paula's hand went to his face. "I promise."

He took her hand and kissed it. "Right, then. Up you go."

They had a time untangling themselves and sorting out what was whose. Then they both stood up, shook out their clothes and wrestled back into them, shook out the blanket and folded it together, and headed toward his car and the hostel.

"Oh my gosh!" Paula shrieked. "Your car has been here all day and all night, and I'll be walking *in* at this hour of the morning looking like mortification personified. What will Alfie say?"

"Alfie will have heard from James that you probably wouldn't make it in last night, but he will be deaf, dumb and blind if anyone asks, as soon as I let him know there's a pint in it for him."

"Great. Ireland—where a reputation can be bought or sold for the price of a pint. What a country!" she exclaimed.

"You haven't got a reputation worth saving now. Tongues will be wagging today, if they aren't already. You are a marked woman,

Paula," he revealed with elfish mirth. "You can never return to Valentia without me."

Tom pulled up in front of the hostel. "Take your time. I have some things to finish up at my aunt's before leaving. A couple of hours should do it. We'll aim for nine o'clock. I'll give you a lift as far as the turnoff to Galway." He was still absolutely in control.

He took a bar of his aunt's homemade Irish oatmeal soap off the dash and gave it to her. Paula was touched. Did Tom memorize every word she said? She got out of the car, threw her head back and walked tall through the door. He could not help but laugh after her. As she passed by the desk, she noticed that Alfie had a twinkle in his eye. Welcome to it, she thought. His wildest imaginings could not match her reality.

She entered the dormitory quietly so she would not awaken the other travelers or embarrass herself any further. The long day—and night—in sand and sea left her feeling gritty. She took her time in a steaming shower. Lathered in Aunt Moira's oatmeal soap, she let the hot water wash over her doubts.

Paula cleaned out her locker and slipped her ID into her bag; her days as an unknown were over. She changed into her trekking clothes, tried to shake more sand out of her others, stuffed the rest of her things into her pack and tied her bedroll onto the top. While zipping it all tight, she found the handful of souvenir postcards she collected her first day on the island. Impulsively she scrawled on the back of one, affixed a stamp, and dropped it into the post box on her way out the door. She tried to give Alfie a cheerful goodbye.

When Paula stepped out of the hostel, she appeared exactly as the first time Tom saw her—minus the rainwater. Her dark hair was done up tightly under a kerchief tied at the back of her neck. A bulky sweater and loose trekking pants camouflaged her curves. Her pack was slung over her shoulder. She still flashed the smile that enraptured him.

Tom was in his car waiting. He looked much the same as when she first saw him. He was unshaven with his face resolute, but his slate blue eyes lacked the same twinkle. He was still in his sweats. A newspaper lay on the passenger seat.

They did make the nine o'clock ferry. He brought hot tea—in mugs—and scones, so their conversation was necessarily kept to a minimum. What little dialogue there was, was stilted and impersonal. When they reached the junction north, she turned to shake his hand and thank him for the lift.

"I understand what she meant now," Tom began haltingly.

"Who?"

"My Aunt Moira, when she cautioned me to be strong enough to accept a little private sin in my life and then let it go. I believe you're my private sin, Paula... and now I have to let you go. I hope against hope I can rescue you again."

She grabbed her gear and slid out of the car. Tom had not helped her into the car; he did not help her out. She was dependent on herself once more. As she closed the door, she threw him a confidant smile and a wave. Then she trudged toward the north and never looked back.

Tom stared after Paula until she was just a speck along the side of the road. Then he gunned the engine of his racy roadster, turned east and peeled off toward Dublin, turning over and over in his mind a favorite line from Yeats about a man loving a vagabond soul. He found no comfort in the shared pain.

* * * * *

After leaving Tom, Paula's lifts to Galway were unexceptional until the last one. Her liveliness was not so acute as it had been; her responses friendly but brief. The brawny young Irish fisherman who picked her up had strangely familiar dancing blue eyes and an unmanageable shock of red hair with full blazing beard to match.

Her reticence caused him to caution, "I hope ye have ne fallen in love with any Irishman yet. Watch out for us Irishmen, love. We'll capture yer heart every time." Punctuated with an impish grin and a twinkle in his eye, his warning came too late for her.

Am I so obvious? she wondered.

That night, as she bedded down next to a hedge near a thatched cottage not far from Galway, a light rain began to fall. She snuggled deep inside her bedroll to ponder her disappointing farewell from Tom. So much had changed her in the last three days. Beginning to shiver from the damp, she pushed that longing aside and flicked on a flashlight to bring her journal up to date.

Assessing all of her rides thus far from a less than objective point of view, she admitted that yes, the ride with the flashy blue sports car was definitely at the top of her list. Tom's was the only name she added—someone she met on the road, left on the road, and would likely never see again.

* * * * *

Tom arrived at his home in Dublin later than expected. His mother was waiting for him. He barely walked through the door and put his bag down before she asked about his trip. He stopped her abruptly. "Your good Irish Catholic son's integrity is still intact, Mum. Now, leave me be. We'll talk in the morning."

He climbed the stairs to his room leaving her questions unanswered. "Bloody Hell!" Tom shouted at the conflicted face in his mirror. His aunt's report of his island assignation *had* preceded him.

He spent the next few days at the office readying for his trip to Belfast. Everyone stayed out of Tom's way, including his uncles. Word traveled just as fast in the big city as it did in the small village. Had he displayed any exuberance or good nature, they would have been all over him with advice and reproof. As it was, his relations assumed that whatever he was involved with on Valentia Island reached a sad but inevitable conclusion. Just as well. He had plans to hatch.

After three days in Belfast, Tom returned optimistic that he had found someone he could use on site if his uncles would agree. He also recognized that the fears for violence both he and Paula expressed might soon become a reality. He returned to his office and approached his desk, now piled with old mail. He had not really tended to anything since his trip to the west.

He thumbed through the mound of correspondence quickly until he reached a postcard—of puffins. He checked the calendar. Woburn had not occurred yet. His heart raced as he thought Paula might have encountered trouble along the way. He turned the card over and examined the postmark—the day they parted—and read the terse message:

> Gidetti's Gelateria
> near the Pantheon
> Sept. 18
> 4 p.m.
> P.

Tom laughed out loud at her mocking him. Why did he waste so much time doubting he would see Paula again? Yes, he had plans to hatch.

Chapter 9

Rome sizzled that September day in 1968. Heat rose from the cobbled streets as Paula hurried across the piazza to the Pantheon. She was only one among many khaki-colored tourists who tried to escape the beating sun by standing in the doorway of this popular monument. Cool air from within rushed to the outside like air conditioning when a door opens.

Paula eyed the *gelateria* across the piazza and knew it would be stifling inside, so she enjoyed these few moments to refresh. She knew she might be on a fool's errand, unsure whether Tom would show, but she was prepared to wait a while anyway in case he did. She headed for the shop, entered and was pleased to find it was not quite so hot as outside by a few degrees. She ordered some gelato and secured a corner table with a good view of the door. She carried a book to keep her company in case the wait was a long one. She turned the pages slowly and soon put the book face down on the table to let her eyes close, just for a minute.

"I hope I'm not too late." Tom's voice startled her awake as he stood before her, formally dressed in suit and tie, every inch the professional. His dancing eyes betrayed an anticipation she was happy to see, and his demeanor displayed an ease she did not expect. "I was afraid I might miss you."

"You needn't have worried. Hitchhiking breeds patience. Did you have any trouble finding the place?" She rose to accept a continental embrace, cheek to cheek.

"No. I made a dry run early this morning so I would know right where to go and how long it would take to get here from the hotel."

"After your jaunt, how did you fill the rest of your day?"

"If I told you that we had an audience with the Pope, you wouldn't believe me, so we'll say that I lunched and shopped with Mum and the girls, and I tried to say 'No.' Mostly I just nodded."

Paula swallowed her gasp and offered, "Let me get you some *gelato*." When he started to object, she interjected, "It's my turn to treat you," with a stare that said there would be no discussion. "I've tried almost every ice here at one time or another, and it's all great. The lemon is tart and tasty and the watermelon is very good, the flavor true to the fruit. Do you even grow watermelons in Ireland?"

Tom sat. He thought this might be a test. What quality did he want to project with his choice—conservative or risky? "I'll try the watermelon, as long as it doesn't have seeds," he joked. "And no, we do not often have watermelon."

As she stood at the counter ordering, Tom noticed how the last few weeks of manual labor in the Provençal sun enhanced the striking appearance he remembered. Her body was toned and tawny. Her skirt was a midnight green, the shadowy hue that settles over a forest just before the moon rises. It clung to the curve of her hips, stopped just above her knees and was topped by a low-cut matching shell. She wore a filmy pearl white and blue-green patterned overblouse, opaque enough to tantalize but not reveal. Its tails were tied just below the ribs, exposing a sash around her tiny waist. Sunglasses perched atop her head. Even though the heat was stifling, her hair was down, gently pulled back from her face. He was disappointed not to see any flower tucked behind her ear.

Paula returned with his treat. "I thought a cup was best. In this heat *gelato* tends to melt quickly, as you can see," she said pointing to her own.

He asked her flavor—tangerine—and wondered what that revealed about her? He picked up the book she was reading, Hemingway's *A Moveable Feast*, and glanced over a few pages. "Is that true... what he says about Paris?"

"I have the rest of my life to find out, but up to now it has felt that way, even after just a few short visits. I'm anxious to see how living there will feel."

"Don't become too attached to Paris. You're going to like Rome too, and Dublin has its own magic," he winked. When she failed to respond, he asked, "You're still with your plan, then?"

"So far. I'm approved for taking classes at the Sorbonne if I can produce a transcript showing I graduated with an acceptable GPA. I should be able to find living quarters through the university if I carry enough units. I also found a resource for employment for foreigners— an outfit that pairs aliens who need work with others who want work done without the hassle of government regulation. I just have to remember to leave the country before my six-month visa is up. Then I can return if I want to for another six."

"Maybe a trip to Dublin would serve."

"Maybe it would," Paula replied as she flashed him a bewitching smile.

Tom fumbled in his pocket and removed her postcard and the paper with the ogham stone rubbing folded around it. He opened the list she had written for him. "I did have a chance to listen to some music when I was in London, a couple of times actually, like you suggested. Some didn't appeal at all. I didn't like Hendrix or Joplin much. She sounded as rough as you did trying to imitate her. I did like Bob Dylan, and yes, I listened to the words, particularly about changing times." He hummed a phrase. "The Mamas & Papas remind me of you." Tom stole a glance across the table. "*Playboy* was... interesting. The photos were hard to avoid. No wonder it is censored, and well it should be!"

"How sinful of you!" Paula laughed. "Tell me about your trip to Belfast. Any troubles yet? I didn't notice anything unusual when I passed through."

"The trip was interesting. Productive, I think. I was put on to some of the more active students, persons to watch so to speak. One of them is a young female student, a bit younger than you and quite a rabble-rouser they say. But more about that later." Tom swirled the spoon in his *gelato*, then turned his attention to Paula. "I'm not sure I want to hear about Woburn. I'm just glad you seem to have avoided trauma. Skip that episode and tell me about your work camp."

"I'm not sure you'll want to hear about the camp either," Paula sighed. "I did get my wish. I was definitely in the minority at the camp. I was the only American and the only native English speaker. There were about thirty students in all from Algeria, Spain, France, Germany, Denmark, Sweden and one fellow from Czechoslovakia. He spent most of his time huddled near the one radio listening to news reports of Soviet tanks crossing the border into his country and of Dubcek's arrest. I think he had family near the action."

She grew more and more animated as she told stories of Lagnes. He sat back and absorbed her excitement as words tumbled out of her mouth. The tales of shared kitchen duties, a bathtub sarcophagus, and digging latrines disgusted him. He could imagine her playing guitar and singing on the terrace of a village café with coins tossed her way, as she described. He smiled at the recollection of her doing just that for him. "You did work?"

"Oh, yes. Eight hours a day. Moving dirt. We excavated an old chateau rumored to have Moorish features. We tried to uncover a tile floor without breaking the tiles. That involved a lot of shoveling dirt from one place to another, sweeping and then brushing the tiles carefully until we exposed them. No worse than other work I've done. The only room which was cleared out was below ground level—a kitchen and dining area with no electricity—so we slept in one end, cooked in the other and ate in the middle. We got real handy with changing clothes inside our sleeping bags. Thankfully we had plenty of water from a well."

"My word! I can't imagine anyone working and living like that voluntarily. The thought of you...." He shook his head and pursed his lips.

She gave his arm a pat. "I managed just fine. I can take most anything for a while, but I am glad to be among the civilized again."

"I have a surprise for you," Tom announced. She perked up. "We're going to meet my mother for drinks at the hotel in just a few minutes." He blanched at the sudden deer-in-the-headlights look in her eyes.

"A surprise would be balloons... or a puppy. I'm not sure I'm up for family."

"You've just convinced me you can survive anything, so you will be fine," he laughed at her foolishness. "Mum's very anxious to meet you."

"What have you told her about me that she should be so 'anxious,' as you put it?"

"When she asked where I was going in such a hurry and if I would be back in time to join the family for dinner, I told her I had an appointment with a friend I met earlier this summer and would not be available. No details, if that's what you're worried about. I could tell by her expression that drinks as a compromise would be necessary to stem her anxiety, so drinks it is. No worries. My relations are most cordial. We'd better get going."

Tom slipped his papers and her book into his suit pocket and grabbed Paula's hand, giving it a squeeze. "It's been too long," he said as they worked their way out the door and across the piazza. "It's only a bit over a kilometer, so I think we can walk it if you don't mind. Hang on."

* * * * *

Tom guided them along side streets and past the Trevi Fountain crowded with tourists. "We'll come toss our coins later," he promised and steered them to Via Del Tritone which took them to Via Vittorio Veneto and his hotel, the Sontuoso. It was definitely upscale, elegant and conservative, and more cosmopolitan than Italian; it suited his family's station. They ascended a short flight of marble stairs to the lounge and found a table. He ordered drinks for them, claret, not the Irish brew she expected. When she seemed surprised, he replied "When in Rome...."

Paula excused herself and said she would be back in a few minutes. He knew he had to trust her enough not to ask where she was going; he could not stand outside the door this time. When she returned some minutes later, she had transformed from "lassie" to "lady." Her hemline dropped a full eight inches to mid-calf length; he had no idea how. Her filmy blouse was buttoned from halfway down and its shirttails retied just below the waist. Her sash became a scarf wrapped casually around her neck and then draped so one end hung down her back and the other down her front cleverly covering the bareness of her upper chest. Her wavy dark brown hair was twisted into a tight roll, swirled and clipped high on her head. The sunglasses disappeared.

Tom did not imagine Paula as conservative and yes, womanly, because he was so taken with the carefree girl he met on the road. He wondered now which he preferred. She obviously did this in deference to his mother, which indicated she was willing to assume her proper place when it was important to him—a hopeful sign.

"You look absolutely stunning," was all he could manage.

"When in Rome…." she replied as she sat and lifted her glass.

Mrs. O'Connell arrived soon after, laden with shopping bags. She placed them on the floor as the two young adults rose to meet her, he with a continental greeting and she with an outstretched hand for a friendly shake.

"Mother, I'd like to present my friend Paula who spent the last several months traveling around Europe. Paula, my mother Mrs. O'Connell, who just returned from what looks to be a very successful shopping expedition." They took their places at the table, and he ordered his mother a glass of claret also.

"Thomas tells me you met earlier this summer."

"Yes, we did. And I understand you are here to celebrate the wedding of one of his sisters. Was it a lovely ceremony?" Since his mother referred to her son as Thomas, Paula would too. Best not seem too familiar, she thought.

Tom observed how cleverly she answered his mother's questions with another question and deflected any inquiries of a personal nature so amiably. Any political or religious queries were deftly sidestepped. She often spoke in third person and with fact, not opinion.

"How do you do most of your traveling across the continent?"

"One has so many options these days, high speed trains, planes, buses, the metro of course in the cities, and boats service the rivers and the coasts. Ferries are quite fun and convenient, especially the Irish line. Were you able to book direct connections back to Dublin, or will you have a layover on the way?"

Tom was relieved that the term "hitchhike" was never used. He did not add much to the conversation. He was having too much fun listening to the women parry one another's advances.

At the end of an hour, Mrs. O'Connell excused herself to rest before dinner and extended another invitation to her son and his guest to join the family. Tom declined again saying, "We have lots of catching up to do, Mum, so we're going to duck out on our own tonight. We'll do dinner another time."

They all rose again. "Goodbye, Paula," Mrs. O'Connell said as she offered her hand. "I'm so happy to have made your acquaintance. Enjoy the rest of your visit to Rome."

Paula shook his mother's hand graciously and replied, "I'm looking forward to it, and I am so glad to have met you. You have raised a perfect gentleman."

Tom blushed. Mrs. O'Connell patted his arm. "Remember, my exemplary son, we need to leave for the airport about nine, so early up and out."

"Right," he said without betraying a glance at Paula, and he walked his mother to the elevator.

Paula observed them exchange a few private words, but when Tom returned he offered nothing. He was thinking how proud he was of the way she presented herself, of how she could adapt to any situation and command it, and of how casual and easy her conversation came even while under a stress she did not show. He chided himself for even questioning that she could. He said simply "You are amazing!" and kissed her.

* * * * *

Tom wanted to dine someplace private so the two of them could rekindle their acquaintance without being watched by his family. "Let's get out of here," he suggested, and they left the hotel in search of such a place. "You don't mind skipping the elegant tonight, do you?"

Paula shook her head and followed him from the lounge, down the marble steps, and out the door. They turned to the left and it was only then she noted the graceful lines of the neoclassic style hotel. He explained that it was the oldest in this section of the city and was designed in the shape of a piano to conform to the curves of the roads and parks around them. "You'll notice your U.S. Embassy up ahead here in a minute." They passed it and made another left turning into a web of tiny streets and secluded *ristorantes*.

He knew exactly where they were headed and guided her into a quaint little place. They entered beneath an arbor of living ivy and grapevines intertwined, the fruits just ripening. The interior was dressed in Tuscan colors and divided into semi-private enclaves by waist-high planter boxes overflowing with brightly colored bougainvillea and petunia. The florid theme continued to the table coverings and dripping candles. They were ushered to a secluded corner that seemed to await them. Tom ordered *abbacchio arrosto* for them both and a bottle of wine. Paula did not see a menu.

The couple sipped their wine as they waited for their food. "My mum thinks you're to be feared. She likes you, Paula. She admits that you are clever, smart, thoughtful and well mannered. She can tell I like you too, and that's why she's afraid. If you were some fly-by-night, she'd tell me to—you know—'be careful.' But her parting words tonight were, 'Remember who you are and the tradition you represent. Act with honor and integrity.'"

"And will you? Act with honor and integrity?"

"Don't I always?" Tom asked as he removed her scarf, his hand lingering beneath her chin as he did so. He folded the scarf and put it in his pocket, noticing how the colors in her outfit accentuated the deep green of her eyes.

Paula felt him stare at her again. "Your introspection...."

"I was just looking deep into your eyes and thinking.... Our children will have eyes the color of the sea."

She tried to mask her astonishment with a casual presence. "How many of these sea-eyed cherubs will there be?"

"Five," he stated matter-of-factly.

Her expressive eyebrows arched upward in surprise. "But I only have two hands."

"I have two more."

"What about poor little number five?"

"I'll carry her on my shoulders," Tom replied affectionately.

She had to admit to herself that the picture appeared quite endearing. "Where will we put all these children?"

"Well, it won't be in Mum's house. Too many breakables for rowdy games of Hide and Seek on rainy days."

Paula liked the image he painted, but she wondered what part she would play in determining its composition.

Their food arrived—roast lamb and vegetables—absolutely perfect. She peered through the flowered vines at other couples, leaning in, their heads close together enjoying their wine and their meals and conversation. She felt very lucky to be sharing the same intimacy as they.

"I've done some investigating. I think I've come up with a plan you'll like," Tom began. "I had a chat with my uncles, two or three in fact. I told them I wanted to explore other options at the network. I wanted to give up my production duties to do field reporting and let my cousins take over my job. I would retain my share of the company, of course, but I'd take a cut in salary. The new assignment would take me out of Dublin and abroad fairly frequently. I thought that might make it easier for us...."

"What did your uncles say to this grand plan?"

"They weren't too keen on it," Tom admitted. "They said their sons were still a bit young for the responsibility—one is just finishing university—but that it was a possibility in three to five years, no doubt assuming that whatever I've got myself into will blow over by then. After we watched the reports of the Democratic Convention in Chicago and the violence perpetrated there, the uncles agreed to let me hire a staff person for Belfast. I think I've found a Canadian who can do the job for us. He's not quite so unabashed as you, but he'll do. He should be neutral enough, not hampered by religious preference.

"I think they agreed to put a man in the North as a concession for refusing me the reporting job, but at least my sentence has been reduced from ten years to five," he added.

"So what is your plan for the next five?"

"Ah, Part B," Tom responded enthusiastically. "If you're determined to go back to school, I'd prefer you did so in Dublin. I've checked with Trinity College and you'll need a plan of study, a letter of recommendation—which I'll take care of—and a transcript showing graduation and final GPA. Sound familiar? The paperwork probably couldn't be completed until spring term, but it's a step. It would at least bring us together so we could work out the rest."

"Quite a plan you've cooked up," she conceded.

"That's my job—determine the essential bits and make them fit into a given time-frame."

"Do I have any input in the formation of your plan?"

"You will. Let's walk and talk." They finished their wine. As they quit the *ristorante*, Tom plucked a blossom from its vine and slid it into his picket.

* * * * *

Tom and Paula found Via Veneto again and followed it north to the Porta Pinciana just outside Rome's ancient walls and onto the lush grounds of the Villa Borghese. Tree-lined walkways fanned out in front of them, each path covered by a canopy of leafy green branches providing coolness even in summer. He veered them to the right and left again past secret gardens toward the Via del Lago. He felt free to imitate the other young couples strolling the grounds and placed his arm around Paula's shoulders, surprised to feel tightness in her neck. "Is something bothering you? You seem tense."

She hesitated to intrude on his buoyant attitude. "I don't mean to offend, but that was supposed to be *your* five year plan. It sounded like a recipe for mine. What am I contributing to this scheme of yours other than myself... to be by your side and at your bidding when it's convenient? You make all the decisions from where and what we eat, to what we see and do, to where I'd go to school, to how we'd spend waiting time for the next five years."

"Have you been displeased by anything we've done?" Tom asked, worried.

"Not at all. I've enjoyed everything, but that's not the point. I feel that I haven't had any input. You seldom ask; you always tell. What if I were allergic to fish or couldn't swim? You listen to my opinions but you don't ask for my help in making decisions. About the only thing you haven't controlled is the words coming out of my mouth," Paula contended.

"You misunderstand. It is not that I seek to control you. The role of a gentleman is to anticipate and meet the needs of those for whom he is responsible. I'm just trying very hard to be the perfect gentleman you labeled me earlier."

"I understand that control is part of your job; it's in your makeup. It's what you do and you're very good at it. You even ordered for your mother, so I'm guessing your father taught you well. If I were to agree to play your game for the next five years, I'm afraid you would naturally control everything, including me. Any strong relationship should be the result of ongoing discussion and compromise. You even chose a university for me, for heaven's sake. Will you tell me what classes to take too? What school I might attend and what I study has nothing to do with us as a couple," Paula asserted.

"But you'll love Trinity. It's the best in Ireland, very strong in the social and political sciences and it's Protestant. It's perfect."

"That may be, but *I* should be allowed to research that for myself, consult you for your opinion, and then make my own decision. You, as my potential partner, should be willing to support the decision I make." Paula was adamant.

"I take your point," he admitted.

"Tom, we discovered together that our opinions and beliefs are so disparate, it is highly unlikely we can ever reach agreement on any major issue in our lives. I don't think controlling me now will help us move beyond that."

"I have to agree with you again that we do disagree. I had no idea that what I find so natural would be so offensive to you. When I started to see possibilities for our immediate future together, I guess I got excited and went overboard. What can I do to restore your faith?" he asked.

"Tell me calmly what you see for *your* life in the next five years."

Tom chose his words very carefully. This definitely was a test. "I see myself stuck in the same job, unfortunately. On the plus side, my hours are flexible which will allow me time to pursue... a relationship with... a young woman of my choosing. I see myself... and this young woman, whoever she may be... working out any differences we may have on such controversial topics as premarital sex and contraception and what to have for Sunday supper. I see myself... and this young woman... working toward a lifetime together. I see us... I mean, myself and some young woman... stealing away for weekends on the islands of the west coast and for vacations on the continent where we will play with carefree abandon. I see myself as a very happy and fulfilled man with confidence in the decisions he makes."

He could tell by the look on her face that he touched a nerve. What did he do or say now to cause her discomfort? Best course of action—answer a question with a question. "Paula, what do you see for *your* life in the next five years? Just as calmly, please."

"I see myself determining for myself... perhaps with the *advice* of a friend... where and how I will live my life. I see education and multicultural experience. I see travel and adventure. I see defining and preparing for a role that will carry me beyond five years—that may be marriage or a profession or both. I see myself engaging in fiery discussions of ethics and morality... probably with a friend. I see myself showing affection in private and in public on a regular basis, not 'stealing away' to some safe haven."

Her conviction bore into his eyes as she continued. "I see myself using artificial birth control because I refuse to be afraid of pregnancy. Since I am not willing to be celibate for the next five years, I see myself engaging in consensual sex... preferably with someone special... as I believe a strong sexual relationship is necessary, as well as desirable, for an enduring long-term obligation. I see myself considering commitment to another person during a trial period. I see myself as a very happy and fulfilled woman with confidence in the decisions *she* makes."

They stopped to laugh out loud at their feigned seriousness. Tom curled her into a big bear hug and shook his head. "Oh, Paula, how can we ever reconcile my two-sided coin with your sliding scale? We are two intelligent people who *together* ought to be able to figure this out. I have faith that it can be done."

They rested under a massive oak and leaned against its ancient trunk. They took their cue from the many other couples doing the same, locked in ardent embrace, alone in a crowd of lovers. Groves of cypress and olive surrounded them, the play of water in the fountains serenaded them, and the pungency of lavender and olive teased their senses.

As they worked their way over the grassy rolling hills to the top of the path, Tom began reluctantly. "I shudder to tell you this, but I have already arranged what we will do next. Forgive me for being so presumptive, but it was before I understood how you felt. Please, won't you join me? We need to experience at least one boating adventure per rendezvous."

They arrived at the Laghetto, a beautiful man-made lake of clear aqua blue water surrounded by faux temples and oak, juniper and cypress. Tom had reserved a rowboat. He stepped in first and turned to help her.

"You're not going to dunk me, are you?" she joshed.

"Absolutely not! I wouldn't dare. Not tonight following every other thing I've done to put you off." He took her hand and helped her in. He removed his suit coat and tie, opened his shirt collar and rolled up his sleeves. Then he took the seat opposite her and set the oars. The power of his strokes took them swiftly across the water. Again they felt themselves isolated within a swarm as he found them a spot near the Temple of Aesculapius and brought in the oars.

Tom leaned toward Paula, reached up and gently removed the clip from her hair, allowing her curls to fall around her face. He arranged them to his liking and then retrieved the bougainvillea from his pocket and nestled it above her ear. He clasped both of her hands with his and was silent for several moments. When he began, it was with tenderness but conviction. "We have danced all around this. We cannot avoid it any longer." He inhaled deeply.

"Come away with me to Dublin, Paula."

She hesitated. "And what do you propose we *do* in Dublin?"

"I propose we start a life together. I propose... to you. I want us to wed, to spend our lives together. I love you, Paula, and I'm asking you to take the proverbial leap of faith and say 'I do.' "

Chapter 10

Paula did not answer right away. She could not; she was too stunned. Had Tom suggested a short visit or even stowing her away on his boat, she could summon an appropriate retort. But this... this proposition was too sobering. She searched his eyes and her heart for a gentle reply. "Love me? Marry me? You don't even really *know* me yet, and you're talking about forever."

"I know your heart and I know your mind. I *know* you better than I know my own sisters, and I know we can make a beautiful life together.... Could you ever love me?" Tom's eyes joined his words in the appeal.

"Oh, I do! I just don't understand what *kind* of love I have for you." She tried to reassure him. "If I were to consider marriage now, it would only be with you. But I have no experience which would help me distinguish a 'marriage is forever' kind of love. I cannot get my head around the concept of 'forever' when we're so present in the 'here and now.' I cannot picture what love would look like at age forty or fifty or even when we're sixty-four. If I can't define a forever love now, how can I understand it well enough to work to keep it alive?" she struggled to explain.

Tom was resolute. "Love is one of those feelings only poets can describe. Some things have to be taken on faith. You feel it or you don't. I know I feel love for you, and the only way to nourish that love is for us to be together, to work together toward the goals we share. A lasting marriage will grow if we nurture it. I have faith that we are meant to share this greatest of adventures."

Paula started to speak, but he interrupted her words with his lips. "Don't say no, Paula. Please don't say no. Allow us this chance."

"I won't say an absolute no," she assured him. "Right now we have such different images of what life together should be. We both need time to bring these pictures into focus so we're seeing with one eye. We need time.... I need time."

Tom kissed her again and was reluctant to let her go, but as all the other boats were turning toward the dock, he plied the oars again and headed for shore. They stepped onto the dock and threaded themselves together, following the scores of other couples to the Pincio Terrace and its magnificent view of St. Peter's across the river. As the sun set over the panorama of ochre rooftops, Paula took the initiative and turned Tom's face to hers holding it gently between her hands.

"Suppose we could bridge our differences; there is still one other major question to address. You are asking me to give up my life, a life I love, for you. So I'm asking you, would you give up your life in Dublin for me? Would you leave your family and your job? Would you give up your voting rights, leave your country and the future you had planned there for a life with me?"

Paula continued, "If you can't say 'yes' with conviction right now, then you should understand how I'm feeling. I need time to get used to that idea. Suppose we'd met in Yellowstone Park and felt the same way about each other as we do now. Suppose I asked you to come to Colorado with me and begin a new life there. Wouldn't you want some time to consider what to do, no matter how much you thought you loved me?"

Tom did not have to answer. Paula could tell by the desperation in his eyes that he could not say an immediate 'yes' and that he understood her torment. They left the romantic walkways behind, descended the hill to the Piazza Del Popolo and lingered near the massive obelisk just long enough to admire it properly. Then they followed one of the trident prongs toward the Spanish Steps, deep in thought, the strains of a guitar welcoming them. Tom took them to Harrington's Tea Room, a renowned haunt of English poets, and ordered a pot of tea. He did not ask; he could tell they both needed its soothing comfort.

They fell into relaxed chatter as they sipped tea and ate biscuits. Paula knew the evening was coming to a close and that Tom would take the road to the left toward his hotel and she the one to the right to her friend's apartment near the Pantheon. She put her hand on his. "I can almost envision a future for us, but my answer at this moment still has to be 'not now, not yet.' Suppose we could come to agreement on a short-term arrangement while we tackle the tougher questions. We'd still be faced with those questions. We'd still need to determine where your coin might tip a little to the left and my scale might slide a little to the right, where each of us might be able to give a little."

"Could we narrow them down to a handful, then, the greatest obstacles to our union?" he asked.

"We could try. Would you be willing to help do the dishes?"

He snickered, "Hardly a major consideration."

"Could you accept us as *equal* partners in our marriage?"

Tom was not snickering now; he was listening intently, with trepidation.

Paula continued, "Could you ever condone my using artificial birth control? If you were to forbid its use, would you trust me to abide by your wishes or would you always wonder?"

Tom was not nodding or shaking his head. In fact, he was not reacting at all. He was afraid of what she would ask next.

"If you can't condone premarital sex, would *you* continue to find satisfaction on the side but expect *me* to live a celibate, exclusive life, i.e., practice a double standard?" Paula tendered. "Could you give up the life you have now for a life with me, on my terms, somewhere else on this planet?"

He froze. What more could she possibly ask of him? Where was there room for compromise?

"Would your family ever allow you to marry outside the Catholic faith?"

Everything else was negotiable to a certain extent, he was sure, but Paula's last query stunned him with the realization that their future was not solely in their hands. Tom searched for the "right" answers, but he had to admit that he did not know them—yet. "That's a lot to think about... but you are right. It must be done. I love you, Paula, and I want to marry you. Just tell me there is hope."

"There is always hope!" She snuggled onto his lap, curled her arms around his neck and rested her head on his shoulder as she sang quietly of changing times. He put his arms around her and cuddled her at length. No one in Rome seemed to notice.

Even if Tom accepted the differences she would bring to their marriage, Paula doubted if his society would. "How I wish we could start off in a neutral zone... find our own morality... create our own rules... not feel compelled to conform to your society's standards or mine. Then *we* might have a chance," she murmured as she stood up from his lap. "There is such safety in foreign places."

"Don't sound so despondent. This is a time for optimism, a time of possibilities, a time to share our happiness before morning parts us again." Tom led her from the tearoom out into the starlit night. They meandered a maze of narrow sixteenth century streets. "Now that you've trampled all over *my* plans, what do *you* propose?"

"I don't know. How about Paris in the spring, before my visa runs out?"

"That's six months from now. I can't wait that long," he complained.

"Yes, you can. We both can. We survived three months without knowing if we'd ever see one another again. Surely we can survive six knowing that we will," she insisted.

"You'll write...." he pleaded.

"I don't think so. We both need time and distance... unencumbered by emotion. Let's just both stick to working out our own answers independently. If our feelings can't survive a little time and distance, then we weren't meant to be."

Paula noted an objection register on Tom's face. "A compromise then. I'll send you a postcard at the end of winter term with suggestions for spring. I'll not enroll in any spring program so I'll have a clean slate and be free to travel, depending on how we feel then."

"I guess I've not much choice but to agree. I know how I will feel. Come February I'll be checking the post box every day."

"You don't have to respond, you know."

"I know. But you know I will."

* * * * *

Tom and Paula found themselves at the Piazza Barberini, the fork that would take them their separate ways. They made themselves comfortable on the grass under a row of trees facing Bernini's Fontana della Api, the Fountain of the Bees. They enjoyed the movement of the water on the beautiful baroque sculpture, an open fanlike scallop shell with three bees lighting near the shell's hinge about to drink the bright blue-green water. The frivolity of the motif lifted some of the gravity from their circumstance. "I'm not ready to say goodbye to you, but I have no secluded beach to be our bed tonight, nor a blanket to roll you in, " he said with regret.

"No matter." She cuddled closer. "When in Rome.... What *do* the Romans do?" He responded with a series of embraces, each more ardent than the last. She returned his amorous advances with her own. Even within arm's reach of the Pope's city, no one condemned them for their shared pleasures.

Tom stood up and pulled Paula to join him. He brushed himself off and then did the same for her. He walked to the base of the fountain, his hands in his pockets, and watched the water arc from the bees' mouths, pondering his next words. She left him to his private thoughts and entertained some of her own. Should she give up Paris for Dublin? Not yet. She was sure they needed time apart.

He turned and bid her come to him beside the fountain. "You are my private sin, Paula. But this time I won't let you go. Not now. Not yet. Come with...." He paused to restate. "Will you... come with me now... for tonight?"

She was stunned. "Tom, we can't.... *You* can't."

"I *can*. I have the freedom to redefine what I believe. I have the freedom to make my own decisions... and I have confidence in the decision I've made. I won't presume to *tell* you what to do anymore.

I'm *ask*ing you to come with me tonight. It's up to you to make your own decision... to accept or reject my invitation."

Paula's eyes and her smile said yes. She twined her arms around his and they proceeded up the Via Veneto matching their gait. They ascended the marble stairs of the Hotel Sontuoso together, having once again found a haven where the old rules no longer applied.

Sounds of live music enticed them into the lounge where a three-piece combo accompanied a young Italian singer whose smooth voice could not hide his accent. He serenaded the guests with a mixture of oldies and contemporary tunes. "Misty" was the song that persuaded several couples to dance closely heads-on-shoulders and arms encircled around torsos. Tom led Paula to the floor and surrounded her the same, whispering in her ear, "I've been waiting to hold you like this all evening."

"Did you plan this too?" she accused genially.

"Absolutely not. I never dreamed we'd be here together." They continued dancing right into the next number, "Yesterday."

"Every time I hear that song now it will bring on a sadness I've not known before," he lamented. "Six months is so far away. It's time to make a memory to last...." They left and took the elevator to the third floor.

* * * * *

Tom was all gentleness; Paula, submission. They bathed away their few remaining inhibitions together. She detected no reticence on his part; he saw pure joy on hers. The rhythm of effort and surrender, effort and surrender was like floating atop the sea, being massaged by the rise and fall of wave caps. Paula imagined the two of them surrounded by the clown-like puffins bobbing on the water and riding its undulations with the calm assurance that they were following nature's plan.

He must have had the same vision, for he asked, "If you won't come to Dublin with me now, could we be like the puffins and promise to return to our island once a year to breed and nest, then fly back to reality 'til the next season?" He gave her chin the slightest dunk. She enjoyed his playfulness this time and had to laugh at his entreaty.

"Please keep me awake," she implored. "I don't want to waste a minute with sleep tonight."

"It will be my pleasure," he whispered softly as they continued to achieve the harmony they so longed for in their relationship of contradictions.

Gradually the mood altered from the early honeymoon they were celebrating to the parting that loomed inevitable. Beneath a silken cover, their passion shifted to probing, memorizing every detail of one another lest it fade from memory before they could come together again. Their hands searched, explored and imprinted in their hearts and minds the touches that would be absent from them. Their caresses sought the subtle things that differentiate one body from another— the hint of a cleft in his chin, the dimple at the base of her spine, his mole on the outskirts of Madrid, the scar under her chin where another boy had handled her roughly. Their hands came to rest where they felt most welcome, and their tears mingled for the first time. They continued in the dark so they would not see the flow. They did not want to see their tears, but they felt them; their dreams swam in them.

* * * * *

Sunlight through the window signaled the end of their sojourn. They enjoyed a final embrace and Paula asked, "Any regrets?"

"None at all."

"No guilt; no 'mortal sin?'"

"Nothing I can't handle. I may have a lifetime of penance ahead of me, but it could be worse. You might never have come into my life at all. I love you, Paula, and I won't give up until we're living in Dublin together as man and wife.

"Right now, however, I've got to get you back into the city before Mum comes knocking," Tom continued as they prepared themselves for separation. He emptied his pockets of her things. He put her hair clip into her small handbag to join the sunglasses she shed for his mother. He handed her the book about Paris he hoped she would not take too seriously. He tied the scarf around her waist and allowed himself a last tracing of her graceful hips.

Tom walked Paula back to the Pantheon. They did not say much. They stopped at the Trevi Fountain, absent of tourists at the early hour. He offered her a coin and kept one for himself. They turned their backs to the fountain, placed the coins in their right hands and threw them over their left shoulders together, assuring that fate would return them to Rome. Separately, each hoped it would be as lifetime partners.

They continued their journey until they crossed the Piazza Rotonda, which was as far as Paula would allow Tom to accompany her. He gripped her hand with a force he had not dared to use before. "I never should have stopped the car and let you out on the road to Galway. I should have just kept on driving—kidnapped you—and not stopped 'til we reached Dublin together."

Paula stroked his face and kissed him gently. "à Paris," she whispered.

Tom clung to her, not wanting to break their embrace. He called to her as she turned to leave, "I'll be waiting for your postcard," and stared after her as she disappeared down Via Del Cestari and turned to the left. He echoed a popular refrain with his own personal longing for the pleasures of yesterday.

Chapter 11

A crisp Colorado morning greeted Paula as she stepped out onto her deck. Mornings were still cool in late May, so she was wrapped in a hand-knit woolen shawl and held a mug of hot coffee to warm her hands. She sat in a deck chair, put her slippered feet up and looked west toward the still snow-capped mountains. She watched the sunlight reflect by degrees the soft purples, deep blues and stone greys of the craggy mountains, the marbled brown foothills below, the golden hues of fields not yet tilled and the dappled greens of winter wheat and alfalfa. The crazy quilt of colors, textures and fragrances reminded her why she had been so content here for the last forty years.

The coffee roused her after a restless night. She could not understand why her discovery that Thomas did still exist in the real world so unsettled her. She thought she had quieted her latent longing for him, but last night she replayed their time together and awakened wondering why her memories seemed so vivid. Occasionally he was brought to mind by an article she read or a news report she viewed addressing the issues which joined them and then ultimately pulled them apart.

About a year ago, a small headline in the newspaper caught her eye: "American Rock Climber Dies on Valentia Island." After a successful solo ascent of about 600 ft up the Fogher Sea Cliffs, the climber was swept out to sea by a wave which caught him unawares while he was posing for photos at the base of the cliff. It had to be the same Valentia, for the article mentioned the Skelligs that she knew to be near the island. It was not until she read of the climber's death that she realized how foolish she and Thomas were, courting danger in their adventure to Puffin Island.

Paula sipped her coffee and thought aloud with only the birds for an audience. "Everyone should have a special confidant, someone to whom you can open up and bare your soul. Someone with whom you can share your innermost hopes and dreams and fears. Someone who will help you find a moral compass and try out ideas without condemnation, recrimination or fear of judgement. Someone who will dare you to question; who invites contradictions into your life.

"Ideally this person should be a stranger, someone who does not know you and therefore has no preconceptions of you, who you are or who you should be. Someone who challenges your sensibilities.

"For me, this person was Thomas," she declared.

Paula took another sip of hot coffee to quell the shiver that was working its way up her spine. When did she stop using the familiar

"Tom" and begin referring to him with the formal "Thomas?" When did her mind transform him from intimate friend to acquaintance? Surely this marked a significant change in their relationship, if indeed a true and lasting relationship ever existed outside her memory.

Against her better judgement, she went back inside to her study and turned on the computer. She promised herself she would not pursue yesterday's investigation any further, but she wanted to take another look at Thomas' bio. She entered the web address and his vitals again and followed the link his TV network provided. She was disappointed not to find pictures or video. There were only two newspaper articles reporting his receipt of the Eire Award for outstanding work in broadcast journalism on two different occasions.

The first was for a piece he produced in 1975 about a student leader of the civil rights campaign in Northern Ireland in the late sixties. His documentary portrayed her as a fiery leader of radical agitators with support of the IRA. Elected a member of Parliament at an early age, she lost her seat in the mid seventies. The award winning documentary was a retrospective of her efforts toward a united Ireland. When the reporter asked Thomas why his piece omitted details of her personal life, particularly her choice to have a child "without benefit of clergy," Thomas replied, "Her personal choices did not influence her politics; her preferences were an outgrowth of them. Our film dealt with her politics."

Paula remembered his mentioning this woman when he first went to Belfast. Interesting, she thought. Did she detect a slight shift in his thinking? One that might have made a difference for them?

The second award was given for Thomas' documentary on the life and works of a beloved member of the royal family following his murder by the IRA in 1979. His death following the bombing of his boat along the west coast of Ireland signaled the level of violence the IRA was prepared to employ beyond the borders of the North. When asked about the use of violence to obtain political objectives, Thomas replied, "Cowardly acts are not those of conscience. They do not advance the causes of those who perpetrate them."

He witnessed the shift from nonviolence to violence used to effect change that both of them predicted more than ten years before this piece was produced. She wondered how much of the conflict Thomas witnessed firsthand. With a sigh, she exited his past and turned off her computer.

The personal relationship forged by their conversations epitomized the controversies that would tear the next few decades apart. Paula began to see their relationship for what it had been—a chance to try out new philosophies and codes of conduct that would guide them over the intervening years. They played with new ideas, beliefs and behaviors, without criticism or censure. These strengthened them and helped them find their separate ways. Their innocent sophistication found a place for safe discourse in a comfortable, non-threatening environment. They experienced a passage from youthful ideals to adult realities. They struggled between what one could change and what one was bound to accept.

Thomas and Paula were searching for their own true north as gauged from the west coast of Ireland.

Chapter 12

Early June in Colorado brought a profusion of wildflowers to the foothills. White, yellow, orange and purple blanketed the meadows and the edges of the creeks. The cultivated prairie lands were rife with the aroma of the first cutting of new mown hay. Paula was in her garden. She hoped that last night's late frost did not take too many of her peas and tomatoes. That was always the chance when planting early, but as soon as the ground warmed, she was anxious to till the soil and baby her seedlings. By mid-July she would have more than she could ever use herself and would share and trade with the neighbors. She had no use for this large a garden anymore, with the children gone, but she loved working with her hands to produce something. It gave her a sense of self-sufficiency, and manual labor still provided a physical satisfaction no intellectual pursuit could.

Memories of Thomas had not consumed her life until recently. Truth be told, she suppressed thoughts of him—especially of their final parting—throughout the intervening decades, except rarely when they were sparked by some event on the national or international scene. During the last couple of weeks while weeding or irrigating her vegetables, she began to recall the few times she allowed him to come to mind.

When she read "Angela's Ashes" and " 'Tis" by Frank McCourt, the books revealed a picture of Ireland and particularly the Irish husband and father that shocked her—a picture so different from the one Thomas painted for her. She could not imagine the extent to which guilt and fear influenced the behavior of poorer Irish Catholics, the part alcohol played in their daily lives, that partners in a marriage were largely remote from one another—masking emotion and affection. She did recognize the conflict between understanding and interpretation versus knowing and following a prescribed path, for that was the crux of their discussions as well. She wondered if "Angela's Ashes" would have been censored in Ireland if it had been published in the sixties.

Did Thomas react with loathing or compassion to victims of the AIDS epidemic of the eighties? How did he report it when its spread was purportedly attributed to lifestyle choices, sexual contacts and permissiveness? Would he protect himself and his partner, and would he allow his children to protect themselves despite the Church's objections to artificial means? She decided his reason would prevail.

When the first "test-tube" baby was born in 1978, she thought about Thomas because he wanted lots of children. If he and his partner were not able to conceive, would they ever consider *in vitro* fertilization, egg donation or any other reproductive method to achieve their wish? Reportedly the Church considered *in vitro* as immoral as contraception since both were contrary to natural and divine law.

Multiple royal divorces in the nineties—couples who should have known the game plan going in and who should have the mettle to work it out—brought Thomas instantly to mind. If royals could not conform to rules and accept realities despite their individualism, what hope would Paula and Thomas have for a successful marriage? Divorce would never have been an option for their own irreconcilable differences.

Paula was in a Target parking lot during Spring Break when she heard the worldwide announcement of the death of Pope John Paul II in 2005. She reflected on change in church leadership as opposed to change in political leadership and the common man's voice in these processes. She thought not only of the usual issues: birth control and abortion, but also other reproductive and life choices such as surrogacy, homosexuality, divorce, same-sex marriage, passive euthanasia and right to life, cloning and stem cell research, and child sexual abuse that were facing the Church and its members and wondered if a change in leadership would allow relaxation of some of the strictures binding them.

When she chose contraception over unplanned motherhood, she occasionally wondered what her life would be now had she not been allowed that choice. She understood early in her marriage that her mother was right; Paula had room in her life for but two children, one for each hand. The Roe vs. Wade ruling in 1973 came too late for her that first winter in Paris. Providence intervened instead.

She wondered what Thomas' reaction would be if he knew their son miscarried before she could find safe haven to abort him. She did not even know if the boy's eyes were the color of the sea. When she admitted to herself that even her thoughts, let alone her intentions, would be an intolerable sin in Thomas' eyes, the fate of any future together became clear. They had shared what passed for truth up until that time, but their absolute honesty and compassion were untested.

She tore up the postcard inviting him to Paris in the spring. And, following the pattern of their other partings, she never looked back.

* * * * *

A light June rain fell on Dublin as Thomas let himself into his office. It would be his office for only a couple of weeks more. He retired two years ago, but in deference to his position and his many years with the station, the management, including his son and cousins, allowed him to retain his office until he was "ready" to give up the day-to-day. He was not involved in production anymore, but he enjoyed coming in to socialize and to pretend contemplation.

He was determined to finish clearing out in the next day or so. The walls and bookcases were empty. He passed his files on to his son. His desk was all that was left to clean out. He gathered the family photos and allowed himself reminiscence of what a fine family it was; they celebrated their happiness and weathered their tragedies. He cleared away pens, pencils, sticky notes, blotters and the citations for his work he never bothered to put up.

When he came to the last drawer, the locked one, Thomas used his key to open it. There was not much inside, really, but what was there was personal rather than business-related. He had years of agenda books—the record of his work—and memorabilia such as ticket stubs, autographs and monogrammed pens. He removed those and placed them in the box with his other desk clutter. He reached to the back of the drawer and pulled out a well-fingered packet done up with a broken, brightly colored elastic band. He removed the band carefully and opened out the contents on top of his desk.

He studied the postcard, yellowed now. He unfolded a piece of paper, almost worn through along its folds, with a rubbing of the ogham stone on one side and a list on the other. He had checked off completed items from the list as he read or listened to them over the years. He carefully removed the remnants of a dried wildflower, wilted beyond recognition. He fingered the old cassette tape, a collection from the Mamas & Papas, and wondered how many more times he dared play it before it would shred itself, erasing that memory of Paula too.

"One more time," Thomas said to himself as he slid the tape into his pocket, replaced the postcard, the list, the flower and the broken elastic in the drawer, and then closed and relocked it. He had time for one more trip to the island before he was too old to make the climb anymore.

* * * * *

If she could find it on Google Earth, it must exist, Paula decided as she sat down to her computer. She promised herself no more searching, but.... Her quest began as an internet exercise and investigation to see who from her ancient past was alive, who was dead and who simply disappeared from the face of the earth. The site she used made her search very simple. She found reference to most of the old acquaintances she sought, ones she had not communicated with for thirty or forty years. No need to go any further... except she wanted to. She was aroused by her recent memories of Thomas and their time together and wondered what of her memory was truth and what, tale.

A few clicks of the mouse took her to Ireland, then County Kerry, and finally Valentia Island... so that much was true. She noticed there was now a bridge from Portmagee to the south end. Too bad. It probably brought more traffic and tourists and interrupted the slow pace they so enjoyed.

She scanned south and west just a bit. She found what looked like a big rock—no roads, no bridges, no birds, or at least there were none waddling across her screen. They're too small to show up, she convinced herself. The label "Puffin Island" appeared, so at least Google knew its existence to be true.

What else could she do to convince herself that Thomas was not a figment of her imagination? His postcards were lost along the way, and the two of them did not take any photos. Even the product of their fleeting summer romance was taken from her. She really had nothing tangible but his name in her travel journal and a few sentences describing their adventures. He had been a "really good ride," and they met up again in Rome in the fall. Everything else was left unsaid—no incriminating evidence left for snoopers to find—except that fateful date in February, 1969.

Facebook was something Paula swore she would never use. Her children were confirmed fanatics and suggested she try it too. "Get connected" to your old friends and schoolmates, they said, with emphasis on the "old." She admitted that she did not understand how it all worked, but one thing was sure; she did not want anyone prying into *her* life! Yet here she was, prying into someone else's.

She went to the home page and found she could "log in, sign up," or "find a friend." She chose "find a friend," and got a message telling her to sign up before she could find her friend. Her mind was shouting, "You shouldn't be doing this!" but her fingers were not listening, so she signed up and turned off the computer.

Time for lunch. She picked some radicchio, arugula, chard, spinach and beet tops, a green onion, two new carrots, and pea pods from her garden. She washed and dressed the salad with balsamic vinegar and olive oil and accompanied it with homemade whole grain bread. She needed brain food.

A healthy lunch may have calmed her mind, but her fingers continued to work on their own. They found Facebook again. This time she could log in and find a friend by name. There were a gazillion Thomas O'Connells, so she filtered by location—Dublin,

Ireland—and found only a few. None of the pictures looked like the Thomas she knew, but one of them looked a bit older and more mature than she remembered. She recognized the eyes and thought, maybe a son. Thomas could have one in his mid-thirties now, perhaps. Her choices here were adding him as a friend, sending him a message or viewing his friends. What does one say in a message to someone she does not know who might or might not be related to someone else that she did not know very well? "Hi. My name is Paula, and I think I might have met your father some forty years ago. I'm just curious to know if he is still alive and if he remembers who I am. If so, my email address is:____ and if not, sorry I bothered you." That probably was not a very good idea; it might cause family discord of who knew what proportion.

Paula exited the program. She needed a snack—another carrot maybe. Forget that. She needed chocolate!

The treat did not calm her at all. Thomas was not her first; he was not her last. And she certainly was not *his* first! What was her fascination with *him* in particular? Then Paula realized it was not Thomas she longed for; it was the *idea* of him and their time together on the island. It was the philosophies they had shared and the ones they had formed separately. That was when she first began to find her own true north—standing on the top of Puffin Island looking out across the ocean. It was not Thomas she needed to see; it was the island. Had that mystical mass of craggy cliffs not invited them to share and bare their souls, Rome and its aftermath never would have occurred. The island held the answer to her ennui.

This time her fingers found a popular travel site and clicked on "flights."

* * * * *

Thomas slipped the Mamas & Papas into his tape deck. "Go Where You Wanna Go" came up—and right now he wanted to go to Puffin Island. For several months back then, when he did not hear from Paula as promised, he thought of her almost every day and whispered a prayer that she would find her way back into his life. But when he finally realized she was not going to contact him, that it was over— whatever "it" was—he moved forward. Whenever he went to Valentia she came to mind, of course. How could she not? But other than seeing her ghost on the island, he tried not to think about her more than just in passing—maybe a half dozen times or so, quite out of the blue, usually stimulated by something in the news.

The violence in Northern Island was a fear come to fruition they both shared. Thomas also thought of Paula during the protest marches and demonstrations in Tiananmen Square that resulted in hundreds of deaths. He thought of her when the civil war in Bosnia and the unrest in Rwanda and the Sudan resulted in starvation and genocide. She came to mind when global protest erupted over the threat of war in Iraq. And he rejoiced when peaceful pro-democracy rallies sparked political change in Eastern Europe and the Berlin Wall came down. He imagined Paula jubilant at those peaceful outcomes.

Thomas watched the development of the women's movement with more interest than would be expected of an Irishman in his position. He realized Paula was not the only woman fighting for her individualism. They were living on the cusp between two eras and she gave him a preview of life on the other side.

Often when he was in London, he spent a morning reading the latest American magazines with his tea, a habit he continued after Paula made him her infamous list. *Ms.* magazine became a regular along with some others. He learned that women felt they were invisible and inferior, playing the part of legalized slaves in their marriages. They worked for peace and civil rights along with men but they had no choices in their personal lives. Their feminism was derived from circumstance—a need for family planning, reproductive choices, childcare, better jobs and pay; essentially equal rights and opportunities in all areas of life. Thomas realized he was part of the media creating a "movement of radicals" with stories of men-haters, bra-burners and demonstrators, even though most simply did not want to feel guilt in their private lives as he often had.

No, Paula was not the "weaker sex" to be spared exertion or decision. In so many ways she was his equal—in one or two, his superior. When on Valentia, he would call her name across the vast expanse of the Atlantic, but she was never there to answer. Did he really treat her so unfairly?

On 9/11 when the World Trade Center came crashing down, Thomas wondered where Paula was. He hoped she was nowhere near the devastation; that she was safe and happy. That was all he really needed to know about her, even now, that she was safe and happy. He did not want his memories to become moanings. They joined in a verbal sparring which challenged his sensibilities and protocols. Safe expression of conflicting views was the crux of their relationship; it allowed him to participate in the voicing of opposing ideas without censure, unlike the sometimes contentious discussions he had with his cohorts in Dublin over the years. When he tried to introduce contrasting notions to them, he was normally jollied back to the consensus view.

The death of JFK Jr. in the late nineties and his uncle's devastating illness nearly ten years later signaled the passing of an era and an idealism that spanned five decades. The Kennedy clan championed causes, social and political, without compromising their principles. Paula was caught up in some of it. Although Thomas could not accept many liberal precepts for his own life, conversing with that intriguing American hitchhiker gave him an appreciation and understanding for those who did. He remembered her tale of the handshake that beckoned her to take that path and knew she shared the sorrow of those whose hands were called to public service by that family with new hopes, dreams and ambitions for a future where none were dispossessed.

He replayed the tape and resang its songs—songs of dreams and sunbeams. He only played this tape when he drove to Valentia alone. No, he never allowed his thoughts of Paula to intrude upon his life or his marriage; they invited him to a safe harbor when he needed to still his mind. He hummed along, remembering music... everywhere there was music... and dancing... on the beach... in the pubs and clubs... along the street.... He imagined Paula dancing, with fragrant flowers in her hair.

* * * * *

Driving was not Paula's strongest suit, even on a good day. Driving in the rain on the left side of the road (she was reminded by the rental car attendant) was bound to be the bottom of the deck for her. She headed away from the Shannon airport and turned south, asking herself again what in the world she thought she was doing. Her children reminded her repeatedly that she was the true hazard on any road, that she should stick to short drives around the Denver area. When she spent too long in a car, she tended to let her mind wander and the vehicle followed her thoughts rather than her intentions. She was determined not to let that happen this day. She increased the wiper speed, turned on the car's headlights and eased into traffic—much more traffic than she remembered.

Paula glanced from side to side at the passing landscape and recalled one of the reasons she gave little consideration to living in Ireland forty years ago. Beauty surrounded her here, but it was so unlike the scenes of her home in Colorado. The palette of her world encompassed the full spectrum of the rainbow. Every color, and every shade of every color, blazed through her windows throughout the year:

blood reds of fireweed and setting suns to the pinks of delicate fruit blossoms, red-oranges of Indian paintbrush to the pastel melons and tangerines in the plumage of migrating birds, golden sunflowers to the muted shades of ripe wheat waving across prairie lands, dark pine to soft sage whose fragrances were as pungent as their colors were true, intense blues of pristine mountain lakes to the azure of a crisp winter sky, and deep purple precipitous mountain peaks to acres of light lavender.

She forgot how uniform Thomas' palette was. The full spectrum of a green rainbow contained the burnished red-greens of berry bushes, the orange-greens of lichen, the yellow-greens of pasture lands, the blue-greens of the ocean and the purple-greens of the low mountain ranges, the brown-greens of the aged thatch and peat bogs, and the grey-greens of the Burren and the coast's rocky cliffs. Underlying all was a solid base of green. Thomas' faith was like that, varying shades of the same foundation, but a firm, unwavering foundation nonetheless, permeating every facet of his life like the rain that caused the greens to grow.

Paula's worldview, like her palette, was broad and embracing. Thomas' was narrow. The amalgam of their two divergent philosophies would have produced a muddy arc indeed.

As she approached the junction with the road that would take her to the Ring of Kerry and Valentia Island, Paula was struck by how heavily traveled it was. Trekking that stretch forty years earlier on the road to Galway when she refused to look back, she was a solitary traveler for much of the day. Now there was more than one lane, and traffic zipped by once it cleared the bottleneck at the roundabout. She slowed and edged her way into the circle of traffic, glancing east and the direction the blue sports car disappeared toward Dublin. Should she loop through that city on her way back? Probably not. She might be tempted to…. Better stick with her original plan, visit Puffin Island to assuage her longing and then fly home before anyone there knew she was gone.

* * * * *

After his trip to Valentia Island, Thomas headed north to spend some time with his daughter Emily and get reacquainted with his grandchild. He promised to do so often, but it was hard to pull himself away from Dublin and, to be truthful, it was a challenge to thrust himself in the midst of happy young couples and their active families. Now that he had set foot on Puffin Island for the last time, could he put that chapter… no, that prologue… to a final rest? Admit it. There would be no "afterword." Paula would remain a specter on the island. He would try to give up thoughts of her. He would not listen to their music again. As he slowed for the bottleneck at the Galway-Dublin junction, Thomas stated firmly as if taking a vow, "This will be the end of it. When I exit the round, I will not look back."

He opened the jockey box, threw the tape inside and bent to close it up. When he straightened to put both hands back on the wheel and his eyes on the road, he was staring directly into the headlights of a car coming straight for him, and he summoned the Almighty. "Dear God, please do not take my life in this way, in this place of all places."

* * * * *

The windshield wipers were whipping full bore when Paula realized she was right on top of her exit. She barely made the curve, then corrected quickly and found herself heading straight into the path of an oncoming sports car. Just in the nick of time it took to the shoulder, and she swerved to the left to avoid collision. "Whiskery old goat," she shouted, pulling back into the right lane. "Probably still hung over from the previous night and didn't have your eyes open," but she managed a smile as if to say that's ok, no harm done. I'm fine. Be on your way and be more careful.

When she looked up and saw several more cars heading directly at her, she suddenly realized she was the one in the wrong... lane, and made for the left one as fast as she could, her heart pounding. How stupid! How could she forget so quickly? Should she turn around and try to catch up to him to apologize for nearly driving the man into a rock wall? Now, that would be really stupid... dangerously stupid! Best to keep going and pay attention to what she's doing. Quit thinking about Thomas and start thinking about the islands.

* * * * *

Thomas was unhurt, still breathing even though his chest smacked hard against the steering wheel. "Damn American tourists! Go back where you came from and leave our roads to those who know how to drive them!" he shouted to no one in particular. He regained his composure enough to notice in his rear-view that the green rental barely dodged another collision before settling in the left lane and continuing south. That crazy driver had the audacity... the *audacity*... to wave and smile as if such fateful close calls were a normal occurrence. Even in the split second their eyes made contact, Thomas thought he detected a familiarity, and in the smile and wave too, come to think of it. Must be the fog in an old man's memory.

He got out of his car to assess its condition. His sudden stop was due to a front tire finding a hole in the shoulder, but he did not make actual contact with the low rock wall that bordered it, thank goodness. No damage to paint or fender. Thomas took a handkerchief from his pocket, removed his cap and wiped his brow. Another deep breath set him to thinking again as he leaned against the hood of his car. The last time he lingered here, at this junction, he was saying goodbye to Paula—their first *adieu*, when neither was sure a second would come to pass. Why did he ever let her go? Why did he promise that once he exited the round he would never think of her again?

* * * * *

The islands that Paula remembered—those craggy, forbidding grey islands—were the last outposts at the edge of the vast blue-green sea. Puffins and rabbits. Music. They played music on Valentia. And danced. Danced on the beach to the music and to the harmony of their voices. They played and sang and danced. She had not played guitar for... how long was it now? Kirin was ten... or maybe twelve when the trouble at home began. That would make it about twenty years. She had not touched her guitar for nearly two decades. But up until then, she played often... no, frequently... no, almost daily. And her children loved it. They sang and danced... all of them sang and danced... or was it danced and sang. Which came first? Surely the singing... when they were wee ones and needed comfort or were being put to bed. The old songs were the best. Then came the eighties. Her children outgrew her songs and her dances and grooved with their friends instead. If her daughter had any idea what Paula was doing now, she would sic the authorities on her. Better watch the road. This was not the time nor place for an accident. No one knew she had come.

* * * * *

Thomas resumed his journey north to visit his daughter, his sweet daughter Emily so like her mother. Emily was his wife's pride and joy, her reason for enduring, and now his granddaughter Meggie was the same, so like her own mother, Emily's fondest treasure. Three generations of women in his family, *his* family, and their likenesses were so striking in all aspects—like mother, like daughter, like granddaughter; yet, he found himself praying that history would not repeat itself.

* * * * *

Tourist busses crowded the road around the Ring of Kerry, a popular route for those with only time enough for a taste of Ireland. The rental attendant admonished her to maintain a safe speed of 80 kph that, Paula was sure, exceeded any velocity she had driven before. Even at that hasty clip, motorcoaches passed her readily. She was so intent on being mindful of traffic that she missed the turnoff for the ferry to Valentia, she assumed, for the first posting with a familiar name guided her to the bridge at Portmagee. This would be good, she convinced herself. A short drive up the island before she encountered familiar territory would give her a chance to ease into this reprise of her earlier days.

Surprisingly, Valentia Island had not changed much in the past forty years. The youth hostel was not where it used to be. O'Hanlon's was still there; Dunbar's was not. A couple of bed and breakfast places were new. Paula chose one and checked in; there was no Alfie behind the desk. After a light supper, she took her camera and a walk about the village to capture in picture the scenes she neglected to on her first trip: the dock and ferry landing, the clock tower, the church, the village itself, and of course the sea, aiming her lens toward the sunset. The skies cleared, and the sun came out to play right on cue.

Paula wanted more... more than just a few photographs. She wanted something tangible to take from the island... a blade of grass or a handful of sand, perhaps. But grass and sand renewed themselves. Their grass and their sand, Thomas' and hers, were either long gone or feet below her now. What could she take that had lasted a lifetime or more... that was the same today as it was when she and Thomas were here together?

Then she remembered the ogham stone, that ancient communicator whose markings conveyed a message to centuries of wayfarers. If she could find it again... and take a rubbing as she did before... perhaps that would satisfy her need for tactile evidence of her time on this island. Paula gave her first such reproduction away to Thomas with a list of "to do's" on the back. He kept it for at least three months, she knew, because he brought it with him when they met in Rome. He had probably discarded it shortly after... silly suggestions from a silly girl.

She found the path she thought would take her to the small aged monolith. Paula did find the stone and took several photos, some with herself beside it, others with her arms and legs sticking out from behind, as she would have done in her youth. Then she took paper and pencil from her bag and kneeled to make her rubbing. She thought back on her day. Aside from the near miss at the Galway roundabout, this had been a very good day, very satisfying indeed. Now, Paula truly felt she was right in coming on this journey.

* * * * *

Morning was grizzly grey, as she expected, but it was not raining. After breakfast, Paula went to the dock in search of a tour boat for hire. She found one that advertised trips to Puffin Island and was soon aboard, skimming across the water. Her pilot told her that not many came to see that island anymore, for no one was allowed on the sanctuary. But he had ferried a recent visitor.

"Old Mr. O'Connell was 'ere just a couple days ago." This reference took Paula aback. She did not think of Thomas as *old*, or herself for that matter. In all her musings of late, they remained just as they were then—twenty-something's trying to find their ways in a brave new world.

"I took 'im out too. Seemed to know right where to put in. Said 'e'd been often when younger, then not so much—family and all— then started comin' back the last few years—just to have a quick look 'round, 'e said. Most tourists—I just circle the island a time or two slowly and tell all about the puffins. But old Mr. O'Connell wanted to linger a bit and actually climb up onto the rocks there to have a look. I was afraid 'e might be slippin' and hurtin' 'imself, but 'e's still pretty spry."

They circled the island slowly. Paula saw the rock face where she and Thomas made their ascent and was amazed she survived. The boat passed the pool where they played with such natural exuberance. She wondered if Thomas' emergency kit were still hidden in the rocks—indeed, if it ever had been—and if she should leave a message there for him to find someday when he was in trouble.

"Mr. O'Connell stayed for a long time, an hour or more maybe, and me here in the boat waitin' an' hopin' 'e wouldna have a heart attack or somethin' and me have to get 'im down. 'E just stood up there—on the top—facin' each direction, then finally turnin' west. 'E stood for a long time—stood hardly movin' with 'is 'ands in 'is pockets—sometimes lookin' down at 'is feet but mostly out across the sea. I heard 'im shout somethin' once or twice, and then 'e come down and we set back to Valentia an' 'e left."

On the return to Valentia, Paula reflected. Theirs was not some long-lost failed romance to be grieved despite the consequence of their last night together. It was a partnership in self-exploration. They were testing the waters of their futures. They were as the fledgling puffin chicks for whom the time came to fly on their own, who stole from the safety of their burrows in the evening and plunged deep into the ocean to find their ways in the world and to create their own personal moralities in a sea of possibilities, both dangerous and rewarding.

Before driving away from the village, Paula scrawled a few words on the back of a postcard, affixed a stamp, and dropped the card in a post box.

* * * * *

Thomas spent three days in Northern Ireland with his daughter and family, absent thoughts of Paula. When he returned to his office determined to finish packing, he was surprised to find the "puffin" postcard on his desk. How could he be so careless? Surely he put it away before he left for the coast. He was mortified that someone may have seen—and read—the card. He turned it over in his hand. It was crisp and unfrayed. He unlocked his drawer to check inside, and there lay the yellowed one where he knew he left it. He examined this new card more closely and noted that the message was the same:

> Gidetti's Gelateria.
> near the Pantheon.
> June 21
> 4p.m.
> P.

The writing was the same too. Only the date was different. Thomas glanced at the postmark and the calendar on his watch, collected his memories from the drawer and left his office for the last time.

Chapter 13

Rome sweltered that day with a "global warming" kind of heat—oppressive from above and reflective from below leaving no apparent means of escape. Paula felt the same pressure, caught between her good sense and nonsense, as she readied for a possible rendezvous with a memory. Upon leaving Valentia Island, it took her only minutes to realize that the summons she sent Thomas was unconscionable, but there was no way to bring it back. She would have to follow through—this time—no matter the repercussions.

What if the ice cream shop were no longer there? It was absurd to think that after four decades Rome would remain unchanged. It was even more absurd to think that Thomas would show up. Puffin Island may have been a favorite haunt of his and she could have been just one of many, long since forgotten, their tryst in Rome an anomaly. What if he never received the postcard? Received it but had no clue who P was and to what it referred? Remembered and thought it preposterous? It was ridiculous to imagine they harbored a regard for one another beyond the borders of County Kerry. In a way, she hoped Thomas would not come; she had no idea what she was going to say to him if he did. How would she explain forty years of silence?

Paula thought she allowed plenty of time for reconnaissance of the area, but when she reached the piazza she could not find Gidetti's. It was not there. She circled the piazza twice returning again to the location she remembered. Still no Gidetti's. How could she be so stupid to assume nothing would change since the sixties? The Pantheon was still there where she left it; the place was still crowded with tourists who looked the same. She circled again and found two gelaterias, neither one was Gidetti's. Which should she choose for her wait? She walked into the center of the piazza and staked out a vantagepoint from the vertex of a triangle that granted her an unobstructed view of both. Would she even recognize Thomas if he did show?

Clouds began to cover the sun. The air cooled some since her arrival; it was heavy with the humidity of impending rain. Great! Paula thought. A sudden storm to mark the first day of summer. No choice but to stand in the rain and wait, for what and for how long she had no idea. Did she not do this before on a lonely road in Ireland, she smiled to herself?

Just as the rain began to fall, an umbrella covered her head. "Allow me to come to your rescue. Are you lost?"

"Not really. I know exactly where *I* am, but nothing else is where it's supposed to be," she quipped.

"Be patient. You'll find what you're looking for."

She turned to the man who belonged to the hand sheltering her with the umbrella. "Hi. I'm Paula," she said as her outstretched hand met that of a stocky distinguished-looking older gentleman with a short, neatly trimmed white beard and the dancing slate blue eyes she recognized immediately.

"I'm Tom. And I've been waiting for you for a very long time."

* * * * *

It was her demeanor Tom recognized first, that determination in her step as she circled the piazza. Paula retained her figure, but her curves were not so prominent. She still had some; they had just shifted a bit. The tawny hue of her skin was gone, whether lost to winter or sunscreen he could not tell, but she exuded a healthy glow. She was slender, if not slight, but not frail. She appeared vigorous despite age. Her cheekbones were high and wide as he remembered. The skin on her face and neck was still tight; there were only wrinkles where frequent smiles left crow's feet. Her hair was shoulder-length now, rich dark chocolate with streaks of sugar-white, like soft bicolor swirls in a finely marbled cake. It was swept back from her face and tucked behind her ears, swaying slightly with each purposeful step.

Once, Paula passed close enough for him to see that her eyes still laughed a sparkling deep green. Her smile was as engaging as ever. She was wearing the same shade of midnight green he last saw her in; she always appeared that way when he thought of her and with flowers in her hair. Tom had too much fun watching her bewilderment to approach her sooner. He wondered how Paula was going to solve the case of the missing shop… and then the rain began.

Styles did not change enough in forty years to conceal that Thomas sported the same broad shoulders and barrel chest. He was dressed very casually for him in blazer and polo, but he still looked every inch the gentleman. His open jacket revealed more bulk to his frame and some heaviness barely evident above the belt line. His beard accentuated the square of his jaw but hid his cleft. A tuft of white hair peeked out from the collar of his polo shirt to meet it. The chiseled hollows in his face were filled with age, and he was beginning to show some jowl. His snow-white hair held its wave, thinning over the crown of his head and ending in short slight curls behind the ears. His hands were pudgy and warm but still strong despite the gnarling of index fingers and thumbs with arthritis. Short white hairs on the backs of his hands were not thick enough to camouflage liver spots nesting there. In fact, all of his hair had turned white except for the dark, serious brows highlighting the familiar slate blue eyes.

* * * * *

Thomas had a calm presence about him, Paula thought, almost a smugness. "How long have you been watching me charge around the piazza in frustration?"

"I still would be if it hadn't started to rain!" Tom joshed. "I enjoyed watching you have no control over your dilemma. Didn't you do your homework? Don't tell me you don't use Google!"

"I was afraid my technological incompetence would catch up with me sooner or later, but I didn't think it would be in the center of Rome!" Paula replied, removing her hand from his. "Seriously, I'm glad you came."

"I couldn't miss this opportunity for free ice cream now, could I?" he asked. "Where are you going to take me since Gidetti's is gone?"

Hmmm. Thomas is leaving some of the decision-making to me, she thought. They could go to the right or the left. One small step at a time.... "Let's go to the right," she said.

They entered Isodora's and found a table. "What would you like?" she asked.

"This is your party. You decide."

More decisions. She returned with *limona* for them both.

Thomas seemed more relaxed than she expected as he started their conversation. "I'm so pleased you got in touch. For someone whose business is attention to detail, I missed the most important one—your name and how to get in touch with you. I felt I knew you so well, I must have known that too." He paused and nursed his *gelato*.

"Allow me to reintroduce myself. I'm Dr. Paula Koyle from Colorado."

"And what does Dr. Paula Koyle from Colorado do these days?" Tom queried.

"I've been retired for two years, so I do just about anything I want to. And you?"

"I too am retired for two years now, but you wouldn't know it. I still go to the office almost every day. My son does most of the work; I just hang around to weigh in on the big decisions." He chuckled and licked his spoon. "Tell me how you stay so trim. You look gorgeous, by the way."

"Why, thank you." Paula relaxed a little. "You cut quite a distinguished figure yourself."

Thomas seemed pleased that she noticed. "When you're doing anything you want to, what is it that you do?"

"I hike. And you?"

"I sail."

"I bike."

"I sail."

"Ski..."

"Sail."

"Swim..."

"Sail."

"Jog?"

Tom reluctantly admitted, "I jog when I can't sail."

"Practice yoga..."

"Sail."

"You're a broken record, aren't you?"

"No, I'm passionate. And there aren't many of us left who remember the sound of a broken record. Where is your favorite place to be, now that you're retired?"

"That's easy. I have my own little piece of heaven atop a hill surrounded by a sea of gold and green fields. A deck goes completely around my house, so I can get up with the sun in the east and follow it all day until it sets behind the mountains in the west. Where do you most like to be?"

"On the sea. I sail whenever I get the chance, at least a couple of times a week in good weather, which isn't as often as you have it."

"Broken record!" Paula quipped.

Tom grinned. "Your daily routine. What keeps you busy?"

"I have a small organic garden, four fruit trees and three chickens, so I'm pretty self-sustaining for about six months of the year. The other six I pig out on donuts and pizza and watch the snowfall from my rocking chair in front of a roaring fire. How do you fill your days?"

"When I'm not sailing, you mean? Office. Lunch at the club. Office. Drinks at the pub. Your favorite evening activity?"

"I usually fall asleep with a book in my lap and a cup of tea by my side."

"Likewise. I'm trying to catch up on some of the censored material I missed now that the laws are relaxed somewhat. A hot cup of tea goes without saying. The place you would most like to go...."

"Paris. It goes without saying. And I'm going to guess, you would like to go..."

"Sailing. Let's try something a bit more difficult. What is your greatest joy and your greatest sorrow?"

Paula proceeded carefully. "My greatest joy is experiencing the change of seasons. My greatest sorrow is that I can't reach out and capture the colors of the sunset before they fade away."

That would be so like the Paula he used to know, Tom thought, trying to catch colors and clouds and rainbows, and shouting across the sea. "Sounds heavenly. My grandchildren are my greatest joy. Whenever life seems a bit dull, I visit them and they put me to rights immediately. My greatest sorrow is that there are not more of them! Do you have any grandchildren, Paula?"

"No. My children aren't married. And I think you just tricked me into revealing more than you in this go-round." Paula sought to savor the lightness of their exchanges, but it was not to be.

"As well I should!" Tom replied rather abruptly. They established present circumstance fairly easily; now for the dangerous territory of past history, he thought. "Do you travel much? How often have you returned to Rome?"

"This is my first time back to Rome... and Ireland too. For the longest time I didn't want to return because I..." and she stopped, guarding her words. Tom did not press; he sensed her vacillate between ease and restraint. "Once I had my home on the hill, I couldn't really find a season I wanted to be away," she finished.

Tom chose his words just as carefully. "When I didn't hear from you that spring, I feared your postcard went awry or that it was intercepted at the office. I worried you were waiting for me on the other end, thinking I had blown you off." He waited for Paula to say something, but she did not.

"I decided it was up to me to get in touch with you." Tom became more serious. "I tried to recall every conversation we had, but no name other than Paula came to mind. I finally drove to the hostel on Valentia to ask if I could see their old registrations. I thought you must have listed your name and address there, but Alfie said the old sheets were long gone." Tom waited again for Paula to respond, but she did not.

"You'll laugh—at least I do now," he continued, "—but that summer I even went to Paris in search of you. I spent a day in a café across from the Sorbonnne watching all the students come and go, hoping to spot you in the crowd, I guess. It was one of the most agonizing days I've ever spent. I had lots of time to think... about how foreign I felt being in that place, not knowing what I would do next. The sights, sounds, smells and language were so strange to me—more so than when I traveled there on business. I was out of my element, with no friends or family to share conversation or a drink with. I was uncomfortable witnessing the familiarity men and women—and frankly men and men—displayed. I saw very few families pass by.

"I closed my eyes and imagined being in Colorado instead of Paris and knew the feeling would be much the same. A break from all the familiar things one knows and loves is a dramatic severance indeed. And then the bells of St. Etienne du Mont reminded me of the church bells of Dublin and how important being true to my faith was to my life. It took me several painful months, and then one very long lonesome day of introspection, to realize that our life together was not to be. I had to chide myself. Here you Americans were walking on the moon, and I couldn't find one silly girl inside of six square miles!"

Again Tom searched Paula's face for some response, but she remained stolid. "When I regained my wits, I prayed that *your* realization of the impossibility of a life together was not so painful or foolish as mine. I hoped, rather, that it took the form of some suave Frenchman who swept you off your feet beneath the pink and blue sky of Paris." He paused and noticed Paula's eyes turn grey and brooding. "Observing you now, I suspect that was not the case.

"A couple of years ago, I tried an Internet search. Do you know how many Paulas there are in the world? In Colorado? I didn't even know where you were to narrow the search... so I'm glad you were successful in finding me... even after all this time. You are a better detective than I."

"You haven't changed your name nor changed your job, apparently," Paula finally replied, tension creeping into her voice. "Thomas... Tom, it wasn't you.... It was... my fault.... *I*... didn't... follow through. It was wrong of me... not to contact you with my decision."

"Right," was all he could say as he tried to read the deeper meaning behind her eyes. He finished his gelato; she finished hers. Neither of them spoke for some time. Tom finally broke the silence.

"Paula, you can't have come all this way across the ocean just for some ice cream and a word game. What is this visit *really* about?" Tom quizzed, leaning forward with his arms on the table and his hands folded. He did not want to seem threatening, but he did not want Paula thinking she could dodge the issue with pleasantries. "Why are we here?"

She cleared her throat and leaned forward, her arms on the table and hands clasped as well. She did not avert her eyes from his. "*You're* here because you are gracious enough to respond to a call from your distant past from someone... who hurt you. I never should have intruded on your personal life like this. I knew after I'd posted the card that I shouldn't have—but there was no bringing it back. If I caused you distress, it is up to me to relieve it. Apology is not enough for my indiscretion, but apology is all I can offer." She waited for Tom to say something, but he did not.

"*I'm* here because of an old woman's silliness. Once retired, I spent many hours sorting through the detritus of my past—you probably did the same—to spare my children that responsibility later. When I got to the 'lost years,' I found lots of maps and photographs of castles, cathedrals, monuments and sculptures, rivers, mountains and boats, but no people. My record of that specific time revealed nothing of the souls who shaped my journey. My travel journal, likewise, held names but no faces. I suddenly needed something tangible to validate my time over here." Paula waited again for him to respond, but he did not.

"My daughter encouraged me to try an Internet search, the last thing I was competent to do. With the social networking sites available these days, she said, I could find anyone. Against my better judgement, I got out my journal and went to work. It seems you are the sole survivor of the species *knightinarmorus europeansus*, era 1968-69. Realizing you were still alive brought back a flood of memories so vivid they couldn't possibly be real. Selfishly I set out on a quest to separate truth from tale, to find tangible evidence of those important events in my life.

"I thought a return to Puffin Island would give me the confirmation I needed, but once there, I wanted more. I took a chance—on a whim—that visiting Rome might satisfy me. I never intended to involve you personally. Again, I apologize for my foolishness... but subconsciously maybe I also felt a need to try to right a past wrong, to stand at a fountain and shout 'I'm... so... sorry' across its calm water." She paused. "Can you ever forgive me?"

Tom studied Paula's face for the sincerity of her words. "Well, here I am, your living proof that we went to Puffin Island together... and we met in Rome for ice cream at a place that no longer exists... and we parted with hope in our hearts. If it's more tangible proof you need, you're welcome to take my picture... or... take my hand." He opened his palm toward hers.

Paula scrutinized Tom's eyes for the implication in his words. She rested her hand on his, and he grasped it firmly.

"Your silliness was one of your most endearing qualities, Paula. Don't ever try to stifle it."

* * * * *

Tom and Paula remained hand-clasped-in-hand, alone in a crowd, attempting to reignite their acquaintance. They enjoyed a return to familiarity as they launched into a new version of their old game.

20th Century composer.
P: Leonard Bernstein
T: Andrew Lloyd Webber

Contemporary folk singer.
P: James Taylor
T: Any sultry young colleen like Christy Moore

Band.
P: I'm not much into bands these days.
T: U2, of course! Dublin's own!
P: You win this round.

Contemporary social and political activist.
P: Elie Wiesel
T: Elie Wiesel, 'though Bono runs a close second and he *is* Irish.

Contemporary Irish author.
T: Frank McCourt
P: Frank McCourt, but he was American-born.
T: His parents were Irish and he grew up in Ireland. He was Irish to the core, and it permeated his writing, you'll have to admit.
They laughed and called it a draw.

Contemporary poet.
P: Billy Collins. He's so irreverent. Imagine wanting additional birthdays!
T: Billy Collins is not my favorite, but I do admire his lines admitting to an old love.

Here's one for you. Contemporary Irish poet.
P: Seamus Heaney.
T: You know him?
P: I do. He tells us to learn from people we pick up along the road.
They both laughed at the irony of her suggestion.
T: How about trusting the truths your senses reveal?
P: That sounds like "North."

T: I'm speechless!

P: Not likely.

Favorite all-time poet.

P: Still Yeats—the young mother who imagines the satisfactions of a son grown.

T: Still Yeats—the ancient wayfarer who searches for his lost love to take her in his arms again.

They both fell quiet and reflected on the verses they had shared. "Do you have any new scars from your many years of adventures, Paula?" he finally quizzed.

"None that show," she replied.

The light rain stopped. "I think we've outstayed our welcome here." Tom broke their hold. "What do you have planned next?"

Paula shook her head, "I never imagined.... I have no plan. For almost the first time in the half century of my adult life, I have no plan."

"Might I suggest, then, that we free up this table and find a more secluded *ristorante* to continue our reacquaintance? Will you join me?"

"It is my experience that accepting a meal from a man..." and she stopped herself, the inference being improper.

Tom grinned with a gleam in his eye and escorted her out of the *gelateria* into the brightness of a late afternoon sunshine that burned through the clouds.

Chapter 14

Tom seemed to know where he was going and led Paula by the hand to the right, the left and the right again to an intimate little place on a side street, Mario's. It was well before the dinner hour for most Italians, but Mario welcomed them just the same and sequestered them in a cozy corner. He handed the menu to Tom who glanced over it quickly and passed it to Paula. She nodded back at him to let him know she appreciated his gesture. Disguising his surprise, Mario went in search of a second menu for the gentleman. Antipasto appeared with a bottle of wine. Before she could comment, he replied "When in Rome...."

Paula and Tom both put on glasses to read their *listas*. After a lengthy perusal, they set down their menus, looked across the table at each other, laughed and put their readers away. They both ordered shrimp scampi which caused them to laugh again at the coincidence of their actions. When Mario brought their plates, he lit their candle. It was not really needed because of the early hour, but its soft glow drew them closer into the table and one another.

"How old were you when you married?" Paula asked, not missing a bite.

Tom was surprised at her brash query, then recalled that she had always been that way. "Twenty-eight. Why do you ask?"

"I wondered who won the battle—you or your uncles."

He chuckled. "I guess I did. My wife Kathryn and I had over thirty years together. She was a wonderful wife and mother." Then his face turned serious. "I've lost both Kathryns—my wife and my sister—to breast cancer within the last five years." He paused. "One thinks he is prepared for...."

"I'm so sorry." Paula was quick to interject. "How tragic for you and your family."

"Yes. Well... we all seem to have adjusted to life as it is now for us."

"Children? Let me guess..."

"No need. I have the requisite five children, as you would say, and they're all doing well on their own. My daughter Emily married a Methodist and lives in Northern Ireland, but her daughter is being raised Catholic. Megan is divorced with two children and is therefore working part-time."

"And how did you, Dad, deal with that?"

"Better than her mum, actually. Anne is a good, Irish Catholic, stay-at-home mother who dotes on her four children. My oldest son, Thomas of course, took my place at the network, following family tradition. He is married and his wife keeps him on a tight leash. They have three darling girls. Michael, the youngest, does field reporting for the our rival network just as I would like to have done. He has been in Afghanistan for a couple of years living his old dad's dreams. He should have a new posting soon, someplace safe I hope."

"If there is any such place," Paula added.

"While they were growing up, I did not treat my sons and my daughters with the same hand. I was quite strict with my sons but more liberal with my daughters. My girls each had to finish university, do one year abroad and work for at least another before I would consent to their marriages, however. In a way, I think you gave me a preview of what I might be in for with daughters and that helped me understand them better. And Kathryn too, for that matter, when she grew restless and.... I recognized some of her internal struggles probably better than she did herself. That allowed me to let go of some of my stubbornness, at least with the women in my life."

His face brightened and he continued, "Let me guess. You have two children, one for each hand."

Paula marveled at his recollection. "You are right." Tom caught sight of a cloud passing behind her eyes but did not stop her. "I... gave birth to two children, a boy and a girl. Both were 'planned' and neither one is named 'Rainbow' or 'River,' by the way." He chuckled at the return of her sparkle.

"My daughter Kirin is in the banking business which is going through some rough waters right now, and she is straighter-than-a-stick conservative. Even you would be impressed. She is my severest critic, my watchful censor and my well-meaning caretaker; it is difficult to tell who has control in our relationship. She knows her own mind and is stubborn to a fault. Had she been my first child, there never would have been a second.

"My son Kurt tested every limit from his first wail. With his complete disregard for rules, I don't know how he manages to run a classroom, but he does. He teaches not far from where I live, and he gives a whole new meaning to the term 'green.' Bless his heart, he brought out a conservatism in me I didn't think existed; in fact, I think I took refuge there sometimes. Family get-togethers are one long raucous political debate from beginning to end."

"Is there a husband in this discoursing family of yours, or did you just plan your children and get on with it?" Tom joked, then realized he should not have.

Paula let his indiscretion pass. "Of course there was a husband," she stated. "Turns out, Ken and I shared a passion for learning but not an interest in one another's passion. Our divorce was amicable but definitive." She said no more on the subject.

"Your name. Koyle?"

"My married name and professional one—the one on which I've built my reputation. Too complicated to change it and start over."

Tom hesitated to ask, "And your brother?"

"Chuck is a pediatric dentist in Denver. He should be retired, but he loves what he does," Paula explained. "About the time he lost two close friends to the war and saw others come home to live their lives in wheelchairs, he realized that our parents had valid reason to push him in the direction they did. He spent his two years in the service in Hawaii deciding dentistry might be his calling after all."

"The Peace Corps?" he pried.

"Postponed indefinitely," Paula replied. "Funny you should ask. When I first retired and my daughter asked what I was going to do with my freedom, I suggested fulfilling a lifelong dream to join the Peace Corps. Kiri went ballistic. 'No mother of mine is going off to the jungle to dig latrines and catch hepatitis,' she objected. 'You're going to stay safe and sound right here where I can keep an eye on you!' She sounded just like her grandmother some forty-plus years ago," Paula laughed. They both saw the irony in those remarks. "I didn't dare tell her I was coming on this jaunt."

Mario came to clear their plates. They passed on *dolci* but were grateful for the coffee he brought. Tom shifted around the table toward Paula until their chairs were perpendicular and touching. Accordion music was just beginning to play in the background, creating an ambiance worthy of an Italian film.

They sipped their coffee, Tom playing her fingers with his own. "What are you a doctor of, Paula? Don't dare tell me you are a psychologist."

"Not at all. My Ph.D. is in linguistics and oral tradition."

"That seems an odd fit."

"Not really. My master's came quickly and easily. By the time I was studying for my Ph.D. I was married with children, a home to run and a job teaching at the college. It took me a long time to achieve, but by the end I knew what I wanted—to understand how ideas travel through language.

He tried to hide a grin behind his fist as he leaned back in his chair anticipating her explosion of words.

"In a culture, for instance, there may be no words for 'fun' or 'love' because those are not concepts vital to the survival of that culture. In a matriarchal society, all the articles might be feminine. In a society with no written language, oral tradition is the only clue to how that social system works, both from the words that are used and the structure of each word. We speak words and we don't understand their meanings; yet there is so much meaning imbedded in every word. We conduct global business dealings and diplomacy and we don't understand the implications of the words we use. We'd better be defining our terms the same!"

Paula was fired up now and her cup was in danger. Tom moved it quickly and let her rattle on, giving up his effort to hold her hand.

"Don't even get me started on technology. Modern communications erode any sense of meaning. We try to communicate with incomplete words and sentences, a lack of structure and punctuation, and symbols and acronyms that can be misinterpreted. It is no wonder there is so much misunderstanding in the world today."

Tom jumped into the fray. "Your rhetoric may have changed some, but *you* certainly have not. Consider the internet and instant communication. If we had had such tools, would we have lost each other for so long? Would we ever have been out of touch for more than a day? Couldn't we have carried on long distance conversations to iron out our differences and ultimately been brought closer together?"

"Possibly," Paula replied. "But I beg to differ. Would we ever have found each other in the first place? Would you have been able to set your job aside for three uninterrupted days while we got to know each other? Would we have been able to disconnect ourselves from the 'real' world long enough to explore creating our own? Let me ask, is your cell phone off or on?"

She caught him reaching into his pocket. A guilty look crossed his face. "Surely you're carrying a cell phone too?"

"I use one only when I travel."

"No smartphone?"

"Nope."

"I can't believe it. I can't live without mine. How about GPS… in your car?"

"Nope."

"The Internet. Surely you use the Internet. Facebook. My Space. Twitter."

"Obviously not very well. I couldn't find you, and I didn't think to use it to try to find Gidetti's. Since I finished my research, I use the Internet sparingly. I know how to book a flight, to check the weather, and to find the concert schedule for DPAC."

"My Lord, you are isolated! Where have you been for the last ten years?"

"In my home on the hill, uninterrupted by the incursions of a technological world. We don't need more smartphones; we need more poets. Poets tell it like it is. Their poems have power and meaning.

Poets (including many musicians) may not be able to stop injustices in the world, but they can open our eyes to them in a compelling way we tend to understand." She punctuated the end of her discourse with both hands placed firmly on the table.

That drew hearty laughter from her companion. "Oh, Paula. Your silliness has no end! You just made starving poets the world over very happy. Besides promoting poets as saviors of language and by extension, the world, what are your causes today?"

"My causes? There are so many, but they can all be boiled down to… keeping the mind/body machine well oiled… being a good steward of my piece of this earth… doing something to make a difference…" They finished her thought together, "…each in his own small way."

Their conversation came to an appropriate lull, so Tom helped Paula up from the table. He settled the bill and they left Mario's headed for another rousing exchange, no doubt.

* * * * *

Paula had not strolled alone with a male companion for a long time. She was always in mixed company, of course, when she hiked or camped, when she joined friends for theme dinners or at the local brewery, or when they all went to the theater or dancing. There was enough activity in her life that she did not feel the need or the desire for a specific man's attentions. She was certain that would lead to more complications than rewards. But moseying and chatting with Tom along the meandering streets of Rome reminded her how satisfying a man's companionship could be… especially his.

Tom enjoyed being near a woman again. Just casual proximity was enough. He did not need to hold her hand or offer his arm to feel their closeness. He was not a recluse by any stretch, but most of his professional friends socialized at the pub or their club where women were not so welcome. The club held special dinners where they went as couples with the wives, but he did not attend those anymore. Any spare time he had—when he was not on his sailboat—was spent with his children and grandchildren, so he was not at a loss for company. But it was not the same as the warmth he felt sauntering in casual conversation with Paula now and swathing himself in the sweet sounds of a woman's laughter… especially hers.

The strains of "My Wild Irish Rose" lured them into an Irish Pub near the Collegio Romano. A boyish excitement lit up Tom's face as he implored, "Let's take one turn around the dance floor… for old time's sake. The evening wouldn't be complete without a dance."

Tom left his inhibitions at the door as they hurried in. He grabbed Paula in a dance hold and they waltzed to the last couple of verses. He found the place in the small of her back where he most liked to rest his hand. Not many couples were dancing to the live traditional Irish combo; those who did were middle-aged or more. The younger folks hugged the bar and watched the "old fogies" with amusement.

A break between tunes allowed Paula to admire the décor. It was nicer than the pubs on Valentia. The interior and furnishings were all in dark wood. Polished brass fittings outlined the bar, stools and many mirrors. The windows were of colorful stained glass, and pictures of Irish writers and poets adorned the walls. A large hand-painted mural of Dublin and its surrounds covered one end of the room. The River Liffey laced through the city with Dublin Castle and the cathedrals depicted to its south and Abbey Theatre to the north. Her eyes traced a path from the theater south again across O'Connell Bridge to Trinity College, where she might have been a student, and a short walk further to St. Stephen's Green, where they never would have been permitted to stroll with the familiarity they were rediscovering.

They still rested in dance hold when the vocalist began "Those Were the Days," the Russian gypsy song so popular in '68 when they had no appreciation for the romantic idealism it expressed or its relevance to their lives. When the chorus began, Tom swayed Paula left and right to the one-two beat of the music. The vocalist brought the crowd into the song with the interlude, and by the end of the second chorus, even the young folks joined in.

The second verse began, and Tom whispered to Paula in tune with the lone singer about years rushing by so fast one would lose sight of his dreams. They tried a polka to the next chorus and moved around the room with limited success. The entire assemblage sang now with mounting enthusiasm.

At the beginning of the last verse, Tom held Paula at arm's length and gazed into her eyes as he joined the lead vocalist in a duet, admitting to growing older but still holding bygone longings in his heart. On the first three drawn-out beats of the chorus, he pulled her chokingly close with his arm behind her back until they were nose to nose staring deeply into one another's eyes. Then with a long stride for each subsequent slow beat, they pivoted in lazy circles around the floor that was opening up for them.

They were the only ones who danced now, and they took up most of the floor. Paula thought they must be making a spectacle of themselves, but it was obvious Tom did not care. As the tempo of a second repeat of the chorus grew faster, so did their steps. Then they stopped abruptly, and he moved her to arm's length again as he belted out the final phrase with a grand smile to her, remembering those days... and dreams... they shared.

Applause embarrassed them both. "You're still able to follow my lead very well... despite your feminist leanings," he grinned.

Paula gasped for air. "It was either that or have us in a heap on the floor... mortified." Tom had not lost his sense of rhythm, the lilt in his tenor voice or his sense of humor. Their foreheads touched as he led her out of the pub and down the road, oblivious of the chorus of comments and accolades that followed them.

They walked slowly to catch their breath and regain some energy. "That was so much fun. Thank you for indulging an old man his fancy," Tom said as he took her hand.

"My pleasure," Paula replied, showing her contentment by squeezing his gently.

* * * * *

"We've come full circle, Paula, just like the old song 'Where Have All the Flowers Gone?' Has anything really changed? What did we learn from our youthful rebelliousness?"

"Dramatic sudden change is usually precipitated by a cataclysmic event like a hurricane or 9/11, but in most cases, change occurs so slowly that it is hard to tell. Sometimes the change we get is not the result we anticipated. I don't think the sixties really provided answers. The movements of that decade asked important questions that jumpstarted conversations which couldn't be avoided. They taught us we have the right, and the responsibility, to question our leaders. We have the right, and the responsibility, to protest injustice to effect change, both socially and politically. We learned that many voices together can send a clear message."

Paula grew thoughtful as they ambled down the narrow cobblestone streets. "The results are mixed. The protest movement in the U.S. was instrumental in bringing an end to the Vietnam War, but it hasn't had the same success with today's conflicts in Iraq and Afghanistan. We've gone from a draft army to volunteer army. Many culture wars began in the sixties: civil rights, equal rights for women and people with disabilities, same-sex issues, reproductive issues. We're still fighting on most of those fronts but there has been progress.

"Drugs continue to be a problem. Shortly after the 'Summer of Love,' the move was from psychedelics to hard addicting drugs. Our prison system is overloaded with drug offenders. Communal living was a short-lived experiment. Sexual freedom and promiscuity were stymied by the HIV/AIDS epidemic."

Tom nodded in agreement with her accounting. "People have stopped worrying or caring about things that used to be important, like hair length. Interfaith, even interracial, marriage is commonplace now. The institution of marriage is assailed by cohabitation, the prevalence of divorce and same-sex partners."

Paula added, "Even how we assimilate news has undergone change. We get different information depending on our political preference. With today's technology we can search for media outlets which support our own point of view rather than challenge us."

Tom considered this carefully. He was part of that media which was not always so objective as it should have been in the early years. He added, "Some of the artists and musicians have endured and are still performing and producing relevant works—McCartney, Dylan, the Stones, the Dead...."

"...Seamus Heaney," they said together.

"In the sixties, young people networked through music; today they network through technology. Then, we believed we could change the world. Now, we're more skeptical; we know it will take time and incremental steps," Paula declared.

"And what 'incremental steps' should we be taking now?"

"We should each try to reduce our carbon footprint, I think."

"What are you doing to go green?" Tom asked anticipating a litany of efforts.

"There's my organic garden, of course, and the fruit trees and chickens. I recycle. I have solar panels on my roof, and I drive a hybrid. You?"

"I'm a big user of wind energy.... I sail."

"You won't let go of that, will you?" Paula laughed.

"Never."

"Has Ireland been affected by globalization?"

"One could not imagine the degree of globalization prevalent in the phenomenon that was Ireland before the recent downturn. Our booming economy was the result of subsidies in business and construction from the European Union, and firms from all over the world centered there. We experienced massive immigration from Eastern Europe which stemmed the tide of earlier emigration to America and elsewhere. Dublin is still a very busy place these days," Tom concluded.

American politician.
P: Perhaps our first black president.

T: Bill Clinton. (Paula's eyes widened in disbelief.) For his efforts to effect a tenuous peace in Northern Ireland.

Irish politician. "Mary Robinson," they said in tandem.
P: First *woman* president of Ireland.
T: You've kept abreast of our politics.

Recent tragedies.
P: 9/11
T: The Catholic Church's abuses of children.

The stark realities of current issues brought them back to the original questions about the sixties. "The important thing I learned from my experiences in those years is that we must be sensitive to others' beliefs. It doesn't matter what religion one is or what race, ethnicity, or political persuasion. We need to be civil and understanding if there is any hope of working together toward common goals. In a global society such as we have now, that is imperative." Paula turned to Tom with one of her fetching smiles. 'Peace and love' as we used to say."

Using an apologetic tone, she said, "Speaking of sensitivity to others' beliefs, I never should have tempted you to doubt. Even though unintentional, that was the height of insensitivity."

"You just made me stronger," he assured her. "Looking back now as we are, and putting aside what we've revealed, do you think we....?"

"...could have made a life together?" She finished his question. "I think the censure alone..."

"...would have worn us down in the end," he admitted.

Paula nodded her assent. "I think you would have gone as far as you could—for me. I don't think I would ever have accepted that as far enough. In the end, whether it be weeks, months, or years, I think I would have sabotaged our relationship; I would always have wanted more personal freedom than you could in good conscience give me. I don't think I was meant to be a wife.... In retrospect, is individual freedom so important if you have no one like-minded to share it? I don't know.

"Has anything really changed?" Paula sought to answer Tom's initial question. "Human nature hasn't really changed. Man's priority is still himself before the global community; he cares more about personal issues than global ones. You mellowed; I embraced structure. We both probably still remain true to our core principles. We likely have more in common with each other now than we did then simply because we've learned to accept that which we cannot change, and we still try to effect change where we can."

* * * * *

Trevi Fountain was just as resplendent and just as crowded as their first visit. The pool was surrounded by people, tourists mostly, but Tom found them a place to sit on its ledge. "We tempted fate here once," he reminded her.

"With a toss of a coin we pledged to return to Rome... I remember," Paula added. They turned toward one another and sat quietly, hands in their laps and thoughts lost in the aqua blue water and the myriad coins glittering from its bottom representing countless such pledges.

"I have something to confess," Tom began. "Not *that* often... maybe half a dozen times or so... I returned to Puffin Island. I stood on our spot at the height of the island, pointed myself fifteen degrees south of due west, and shouted along the great circle route to you. Whenever I had something I couldn't work out for myself... something on my mind which wouldn't resolve itself... whenever I needed a different perspective to help sort things out... I'd come and have a chat... a discourse with a memory... just to help me see things in a different way. I'd replay our conversations in my head looking for help or advice. Sometimes I just needed someone to talk to who wouldn't pass judgement, and sometimes I needed counsel beyond that available to me."

Paula was silent as he resumed. "Once I tried it out, I rather liked the sound of my voice speaking, *saying* what I felt. I forgot that Irishmen could express their feelings with something other than anger or despair. I don't think I really expected any answers, but I always felt better for asking the questions.

"One time you told me to *play* with my children more. Another time.... It wasn't so much 'What would Paula say? What would Paula do?' I just tried to recall a bit of shared wisdom that applied. I sought the wisdom we found together."

Paula watched Tom struggle to continue. "Only once early on did I try to imagine our life together—what it would have been—realistically. I imagined us having children. Our first would be a son, of course. I tried to see his face, the color of his eyes, but I couldn't. A cloud passed turning the horizon grey. I took that as a sign I mustn't waste my time imagining what would never be; rather I must concentrate on what I did have."

Tom changed position so he could gauge Paula's reaction more easily and noticed her face turn ashen for a moment. He plunged ahead. "Just a week or so ago I returned for what I told myself would be the last time; it's not that easy for me to climb onto the island anymore. I wished for a sign—anything that would tell me you were real, that our conversations were real, that the feelings we shared were real and not just a figment of my imagination. I shouted across the sea for a symbol. This last time I, too, wanted more tangible proof that I was not clinging to false memory.

"And then your postcard came. It took forty years; yet it seems like only yesterday we were together in this same place, our hearts and our minds in conflict. We may have changed with the times in many respects, but in the most important ones I don't see *we've* changed at all. On the other hand, what appeared so insurmountable then seems so possible now. The questions that divided us then are still the same, but I suspect the answers are so very different. I always harbored a faith... that someday our differences would be resolved. My faith implies transformations and second chances."

Paula was stunned by his admissions. She could think of nothing to say in reply, but her face betrayed her emotions. She dared to reach out and lay a hand on top of his. She curled her fingers around his palm until he grasped and massaged them.

Tom was suddenly calm and confident. He knew exactly where he would take her next. "Are you up for a climb, or should we take a taxi?" Her eyes shot him a dare-you-even-ask look, so he put his arm around her shoulder as they made their way northward.

They strolled at a pace that suited them both. Paula's hand reached up to lace through Tom's fingers dangling over her shoulder. They headed for Piazza del Popolo and the Borghese Gardens. Their manner with one another was familiar and relaxed, and their conversation flowed as easily as it had those many years ago.

As they passed the Spanish Steps, they heard a group of students singing and playing guitar. The music had popularized Ecclesiastes 3:1 in their day, "To every thing there is a season, and a time to every purpose under the heaven." The couple took the opportunity to enjoy the message and the providential moment.

* * * * *

The sun was threatening to set behind St. Peter's on the longest day of the year, heralding change from one season to another. They reached the Laghetto as the sun's golden rays splayed out across the aquamarine water, gilding its surface. Again, Tom rowed them across the lake with the same strength... but not the same speed. No need to hurry now—they had all the time in the world. No deadlines in front of them. No expectations. No inevitabilities.

He reflected on their first meeting in Rome. What made him think he knew anything about love? A naïve young man, who kept his emotions locked in his belly as he was taught, had no business presuming love for himself or anyone else. How many times did he say, "I love you" and in truth not understand the meaning of those words?

Now—with the maturity of four more decades and after marriage and a family, a career defending his church while personally tailoring its teachings, visiting the continent and always returning home anxiously to his beloved Ireland despite all its foibles, and nursing his wife for the last three years of her life—now he knew what "forever" love meant.

"I don't know whose guardian angel brought us together on Puffin Island the first time, nor whose angel guided us together again, nor which mischievous leprechaun contrived to tease us into imagining we could buck society's conventions and 'live happily ever after.' I do know that we both appear to have lived the lives that were meant for us.... But our lives aren't over, Paula. There's dance left in us yet. So, what will be the end of our story?"

Tom stopped rowing and allowed the soothing sound of water swilling over the oars to lull them into shared reverie. "Happiness is so transient; we dare not take a moment for granted.... I still do need you, Paula, and we're both beyond sixty-four.

"I'll never ask you why... why you didn't send for me... why you waited so long. I don't need to know why. I just need to look into your eyes and feel the regard with which you accept my hand to sense that a kind of love still lingers between us."

He tucked a curl behind her ear and ran a finger lightly along the contour of her face and under her chin. "Come away with me to Dublin, Paula," he smiled.

There was surprise in her pause as she considered her response carefully. "I seem to recall we had this conversation long ago." With a sauciness he had not enjoyed in over forty years, Paula asked, "And what, sir, would you propose we *do* in Dublin?"

Tom took her hand in both of his and held it for several seconds, locking her deep green eyes in a confident gaze with his slate blue ones. Then, in a very gentlemanly manner, like an episode from a Victorian romance novel she thought, he raised her hand to his lips and kissed it tenderly.

What's next for Paula and Tom?
Find out in *Celtic Compass, Part I,*
a novel by Sherry Schubert, currently available.

AWARD WINNING AUTHOR SHERRY SCHUBERT, named 2012 Writer of the Year by Idaho Writer's League and a recipient of an Editors' Choice award from Idaho Author Awards, is a graduate of the University of California at Berkeley, Class of 1967. Subsequently, she spent two years hitchhiking abroad, gathering grist for stories and a packful of dreams. "Life" called her back to her home state of Idaho where she raised a family and taught teenagers to solve quadratic equations.

Ms. Schubert's yen to write fiction during retirement is precipitated by her daughter's observation, "I have no idea who you were before you were Mom." The author specializes in fiction that appeals to contemporary women from Baby Boomers to their children.

Puffin Island relates how the historical events and social issues of the Sixties shaped the author and still reverberate in her children's lives today. *Celtic Compass, Part 1,* applies her experience in a "blended family" of the Sixties—before that term was coined—to present-day realities. *Celtic Compass, Part II,* explores the challenge of divided loyalties faced by members of a blended family in a time of crisis. *Celtic Circle~for Better, for Worse* examines how antagonistic members of a blended family channel their bitterness and grief. In *Celtic Circle~Forever,* hostile members of a blended family seek pathways to reconciliation following tragedy.

In addition to her five novels, Ms. Schubert is a contributing author to short story anthologies, *Hauntings from the Snake River Plain* and *Family Recipes from the Snake River Plain.* All of her works are available as ebooks or paperbacks from www.amazon.com or www.sunwaypress.com.

Sherry continues to live and write on the family farm. For the record, she did shake the hand of President Kennedy, and she did play the guitar… badly.